The
TWILIGHT ESCORT AGENCY

By

Bryon Williams

The Twilight Escort Agency

Copyright © BRYON WILLIAMS 2009

First published by Zeus Publications 2009

The National Library of Australia Cataloguing-in-Publication

Williams, Bryon Thomas

The Twilight Escort Agency
ISBN:978-06484238-2-9

Subjects: Fiction--Australian humour–comedy

Cover design – Bryon Williams and Helen Morgan

Dedication

For Gail and Ian;
old friends and 'escorts' who will forever remain young
in my memories and my heart.

By the same author

The Grumpy Old Withered of Oz

Code Name Millicent: The Cat Intelligence Agent Who
Came in From the Cold

The Tourist from the Light

The Burning Boy

bryonwilliams@tpg.com.au

Chapter 1

'Good morning, Twilight Escorts,' Ms Estelle Twigden purred as she answered the phone in her 'professional' voice. Well, she tried to purr but it somehow came out more like a low growl. Estelle was now in her late fifties, unnaturally prim and proper, as she would have been described in her younger days. But on the inside she was, in actual fact, anything but prim or proper. And now, in her later years, after a lifetime of enslavement caring for her hypochondriacal mother, who had finally been admitted to a nursing home, she was at last able to blossom into the loyal, reliable, disciplined, caring, passionate, but sexually frustrated romantic she had hidden from the outside world for her entire life.

Her mother – 'the old chook', as Aubrey, Estelle's boss, secretly referred to her – after years of crying wolf, finally lost the remaining chickens from her barn and was found by the neighbourhood constabulary, sitting in the local McDonald's, stark naked and screaming obscenities at some poor old codger who was trying to show her his Quarter Pounder.

'No, no!' she lashed out belligerently, 'I ordered a Big Whopper, not a fucking Junior Burger!'

The only vacancy that could be found was in the 'We Care for You' Nursing Home for the Disturbed, which

Mother referred to as the 'We-couldn't-give-a-shit House'.

Estelle was slim, but wiry, with a figure more like a second hand than an hourglass. The only time she'd worn an uplift padded bra, she lost her balance and fell flat on her face, almost fracturing her hip. Since then she returned to what she referred to as her 'boyish' figure, or in her case, the now-fashionable Auschwitz look. She had dark brown eyes that tended more towards a spaniel than a Jack Russell, camouflaged by large, horn-rimmed glasses. Her predominantly grey-streaked hair was pulled back severely off her face and held by a brown suede Alice band. She always wore dark, conservative clothes, which fortunately disguised the figure beneath, and the compulsory low-heeled, black court shoes. Overall her appearance gave the correct impression of a rather stern, humourless businesswoman. But beneath the colourless exterior there beat a heart of soft gold.

'Yes, Mrs Trabert,' she said into the phone, 'dinner and the theatre, Saturday night.' Estelle wrote the details down on her pad. 'And what time would you like to be picked up? – And what attire would you prefer? – Oh, it's opening night – Formal? – That should be fine. I'll just have to see if Raoul is available of course and call you back. If he's engaged for Saturday, would any other escort be suitable, like Alexander or Joachim? – I see, yes, Raoul is very charming, and amenable, but he is also quite in demand, you know. – Of course. Well, I'll be in touch as soon as I find out. Thank you for calling, Mrs Trabert. Goodbye.'

Estelle hung up the phone and pounded a few keys on her computer just as Penny Pryce entered the office through the front door, carrying a large fashionable handbag. 'Hi, ET,' she said. 'Got the lunch. They'd run out of tuna so I got you anchovy paste and salad. Okay?'

By Estelle's expression, it was definitely *not* okay but she declined to comment. Instead she picked up the phone and punched in a few numbers that she'd got from her computer record and waited for the number to answer. Penny bounced back to her own desk, placing the lunch bag on Estelle's desk as she passed, opened her own lunch, a serving of chicken and fried rice, and retrieved a copy of *Sex and Celluloid* celebrity magazine from her handbag. She flopped down on her chair, opened the magazine and her lunch, and hoed into both.

Penny Pryce was what Estelle described as a 'young English person' of dubious background, lacking in class, extremely pretty in a conventional sort of way, she supposed, with fashionably messy, shoulder-length blonde hair, which looked like it had never been in the same vicinity as a comb, and featured an alarming streak of bright blue hanging down to her chin. Estelle thought it made her look as if someone had dropped a bottle of ink on the top of her head and it had run down one side. Her bright pink top didn't quite reach her waist, leaving a strip of tanned flesh showing between it and the top of her white mini skirt, slung indecently low on her hips. This in itself Estelle disapproved of, but the hint of a red thong, the tattoo of a crocodile with its jaws open and slavering, pointing towards her left buttock, and a silver Balinese navel ring, did nothing, in Estelle's view, to improve the look. The white calf-length boots clinging to her shapely tanned legs completed the picture, which Estelle thought made her look like a tart. Most men thought she looked more like a scrumptious cupcake.

Penny had been what Estelle described initially as 'an unfortunate choice' as a receptionist-cum-girl Friday, but the final decision had not been left in her hands. Mr Charles, Mr Aubrey's partner, had insisted they hire her as it would give the business what he called 'FOA': Front Office Appeal. Estelle certainly wasn't of the opinion that Penny provided the sort of FOA suitable for the type of clients they attracted. Besides, Penny was allegedly Mr Charles' 'niece', which Estelle considered extremely dubious, but since Mr Charles' family were also from England, it was, she supposed, quite possible. And Penny had developed a not-unusual feature for a Cockney: the overriding flavour of a most alarming Australian accent. Still, Mr Charles was one of the bosses and the decision was his and Mr Aubrey's. Secretly, although she tried to hide it, Estelle, against her better judgment, had grown rather fond of Penny and her bright, cheerful presence.

'Hello, Fred,' Estelle said into the phone. 'Mrs Trabert would like to book you for Saturday night for dinner at The Balaton, followed by the opening night of *Lady Windermere's Fan*. – No, *fan*, Fred, not fanny. – It's not a strip club, it's a revival of an old classic,' she said patiently. 'And do try not to go to sleep this time. You were lucky she didn't notice when you escorted her to the ballet last time. – Yes, well, I know she dropped off as well but she was paying. – Black tie, I'm afraid, Fred. – Yes, I know, it makes you uncomfortable but after all, she is the client and has the right to stipulate dress code. I'll arrange for the formal hire and you can dress here as usual, so we can check you out. I'll confirm the details by email, all right?'

Fred, or Raoul as was his adopted 'professional' name for the agency, was obviously still rattling on about having to wear formal gear and Estelle finally was forced to cut him short. 'Yes, I know. – Well, look at it this way, it gives you a night out and remember, it does augment your pension, so be nice to her.'

Estelle hung up the phone, remarking to Penny as she entered the booking into the Client File on her computer, 'Silly old fool, I don't know what she sees in him. This is her third booking with him.'

Penny looked up from yet another article about Tom Cruise and Katie Holmes. 'Maybe he's got a big donger,' she remarked matter-of-factly.

Estelle scowled disapprovingly. 'Don't say donger, please, Penny. Penis is much more refined.'

'No,' Penny explained patiently, 'penis is average and donger is a whopper.'

'Well, whatever,' replied Estelle dismissively. 'I'm just not up with these modern terms and I'm not sure I approve.'

'That's why I'm here,' explained Penny in the same rather patronising manner, 'to get you up to date. So, next time you have to interview a prospective employee, you say "Now I'll just need to take down your measurements. Height, weight, and what's the size of your donger?" '

Estelle actually sucked her teeth in disapproval. 'Thankfully, interviewing prospective employees is not a part of my office duties any more. No thank you, I'll leave that to Mr Charles and Mr Aubrey.'

'You seemed to get into the swing of it at the auditions,' Penny smiled cheekily. 'Where are they, by the way?'

'Out to lunch.'

'Well. That's the last we'll see of them for the afternoon,' Penny replied, returning to Tom and Katie.

'No, Mr Charles has got an interview with a – ' Estelle checked her diary '– a Ms Therese Singleton, at three, so when you've finished your lunch, will you please give the formal hire company a ring and book Fred's outfit? They have his size on file.'

'Right, an' I'll make sure they put a larger gusset in the crotch for him, shall I?' giggled Penny, then added, 'This Ms Singleton, are we taking on more escorts?'

10

'It's to replace Georgiana-nee-Gertrude,' Estelle reminded her. 'She's in hospital having a hysterectomy.'

'Well, she'll never miss it now, will she? After six kids and at her age, it's probably a bit frayed by now.' As an after-thought, she added, 'Will that come under Work Cover?'

'Don't be silly, Penny, you well know that sex is not included in our services.'

'Oh yeah,' replied Penny cynically. 'I can imagine. You mean to tell me …'

But Estelle cut her off with a quote from their website and the brochure, which she held up for Penny to read. *'Sex is not a part of our service and is only tolerated by mutual, private consent, and on the condition that no money or expensive gifts change hands in the process. Our staff are clean-living, caring escorts and not prostitutes.'*

'Yeah, right,' said Penny. 'I wonder how Gordon, I mean, Philippe got that new car of his.'

'He said he cashed in some of his superannuation shares.'

'I'll bet he cashed in on something,' Penny muttered, returning again to her gossip mag.

Just then the front door opened and Charles and Aubrey entered. While Charles had obviously imbibed a little lunch with his wine, Aubrey remained as conservative in manner as was his mid-grey, wool-and-polyester suit, white shirt and maroon-striped tie that adorned his slightly chubby body, which complimented

11

his chubby face, the cheeks of which displayed a certain ruddy quality, not entirely due to the sun.

Charles called a greeting, perhaps a little louder than necessary, as was his outfit: white slacks hugging, for his age, a fairly fit and tanned body, and a bright, Hawaiian sports shirt featuring a volcano, several pineapples and a parrot. The shirt was provocatively, he thought, open down to the second coconut-shell button, just short of revealing the flesh-coloured, elastic-and-bone waist pincher with pockets, which he referred to as his money belt and which Estelle referred to as his corset. The shirt opening displayed a grey, stubbled chest that was obviously well past waxing or shaving time, and gave the effect of an after-eleven-o'clock shadow. The eyes were still a sparkling blue, although now age puffed around their extremities, with tiny laugh wrinkles at their corners. The teeth were remarkably white and even, due to the fortune that had been spent on dental cosmetic enhancing and regular peroxide rinses, and they flashed as he called, 'Hello, my little darlings,' in a manner that suggested he hadn't seen the two ladies for at least a month when in fact it had only been a couple of hours.

'Mr Charles,' said a slightly disapproving Estelle. 'Remember you have an interview with Therese Singleton at three.'

'Of course,' said Charles. 'And I'm *so* looking forward to it. What a good, efficient, and might I say, devilishly attractive little woman you are. What would we do without you?' And turning directly to Aubrey he asked, 'Don't suppose you'd like to do it, Aubs?'

'Oh, n-no Charles,' Aubrey stammered. 'I've got some, er, reports to go through. And anyway, you're so much better at interviewing than I am.'

'Of course!' said Charles. And then in *sotto voce*, as he passed on his way to his office, 'After all, you interviewed Estelle, didn't you? – And employed her.'

Aubrey actually blushed and escaped, a little unsteadily, into his office.

Chapter 2

Aubrey and Charles had accidentally renewed their boyhood acquaintance while Aubrey was in London, where they were both attending a Real Estate convention. They hadn't actually seen or spoken to each other for forty years prior to that, but the relief of suddenly finding someone at an otherwise painfully boring gathering who shared a past history of youthful experiences was a huge relief to them both. They clung to each other's company for the entire evening, catching up on the past and reliving tales, many embellished, of their schooldays, and enjoyed each other's company to such an extent, they decided to escape to a nearby bar to continue their reminiscences.

Aubrey had been born in Melbourne. His father had unfortunately died in childbirth, which was unusual to say the least. His mother, Daisy, a rather independent young woman for those days, had a leaning toward all things natural, and had insisted that the baby be born at home. The father, John, a rather nervous, insignificant type, was ordered to be present at the birth to witness the torture he had put his wife through, despite her not reaching an orgasm at the conception, which she never tired of relating to anyone who would listen, and to dissuade him from any future ideas of co-habiting and certainly breeding. After the extremely long and exhausting pre-birth agony, accompanied by demands for towels, hot water, drugs, much screaming and foul language from Daisy, the baby's head finally crowned. This frightening and bloody sight caused John to scream even louder than the suffering mother and, clutching his chest, succumbed to a rather nasty heart attack, collapsing on the floor and dropping dead on the spot. This unexpected interruption did, however, subdue Daisy's screams somewhat.

Fortunately, John, who had taken the responsibility of impending fatherhood very much to heart, had also taken out a very large life insurance policy only the week before, which left Daisy and her newborn son rather better off than they had been previously, and furthermore, free of any future bothersome demands for premiums.

To her credit, Daisy did attempt to be a good mother for the first few years of Aubrey's life, but eventually found the joys of motherhood rather tiresome and restricting to her previous joyful independence and freedom, and longed for an alternative lifestyle closer to nature. So when Aubrey was old enough she shipped him off to a rather expensive boarding school, changed her name to Pomegranate, and ran away from home to join a group of hippies in the Dandenong Mountains just outside Melbourne.

Deprived of a loving home life, Aubrey turned to academia and flourished. He eventually won a scholarship to Timbertop, an exclusive boys' boarding school in Victoria, under the auspices of Geelong

Grammar, attended at the time by Prince Charles, and there he was befriended by the less regal Charles Wellington. It was an unlikely friendship, Charles being a naturally inclined extrovert and Aubrey, studious and inexperienced in the finer arts of social charm, deception and skulduggery. But Charles found in Aubrey a loyal follower who delighted in Charles' outrageous exploits, was invaluable in helping him with his assignments, and was always good for a loan to tide him over until his next meagre monthly allowance arrived from England.

Aubrey also delighted in receiving the many and regular postcards from his mother, who had happily taken to travelling the world in search of excitement: Rio, Paris, Rome and even some from towns and cities in Africa he'd never heard of, whilst she was accompanying some big game hunter on safari. Although he marvelled at her exciting travels, he sometimes worried about her obvious restlessness and finally came to the conclusion that, although irresponsible, it was obvious that she really missed him and secretly needed him to look after her in her fast approaching dotage. Daisy, or Pomegranate, on the other hand, was perfectly happy and absolutely ignored any ties to bind her, going to extraordinary lengths to avoid any intrusions in her profligate life, even to the extent of trying never to be in the same country at the same time as her restrictive and overprotective, if loving, son.

After Timbertop, where his parents were furious that he had not befriended the future King of England,

Charles returned to the family estate in Kent. Unfortunately, the estate was completely unmanageable due to lack of maintenance, ability and finances, which had been whittled away by death duties and his father's constant gambling and liaisons with women of a decidedly lower class.

Charles drifted from one unsuitable occupation to the next, never quite finding his niche in the world of business until he married and, through family connections, he was eventually offered a lowly position in Swindon's Bank, Real Estate division. His father and mother eventually died and the estate fell into the hands of the National Trust, and now delighted weekend trippers ogled the now-returned paintings and *objets d'art* his father had previously hocked to support their unsustainable lifestyle.

'It's *so* good to see you again, Aubs,' said Charles as they sipped their Dimple scotch at the bar of the Crown and Castle. 'Tell me, how's the old mater doing? Is she still alive?'

'Oh, yes, very much so, I'm afraid,' and then quickly correcting himself, 'I mean, yes. As a matter of fact, that's what I'm actually doing over here.'

'How so, old man? I thought you'd come over for the beastly convention.'

'Only partly,' replied Aubrey. 'Mother hasn't changed, I'm afraid. I've tried to get her to come to her senses.' He sighed, morosely. 'She actually returned to Australia once to go on a roo cull and fell off the horse. There was a photo in the newspapers: "Old Roo Shooter Bites the

Dust". She even made it onto *A Current Affair* on television. Otherwise I wouldn't have known she was even in the country. Naturally I flew to her side to help. She claimed she was glad to see me, and I thought I'd finally got through to her when she agreed to let me install her in a particularly nice retirement village – "The Hasty Haven". She had her own ensuite apartment, a balcony overlooking a lovely garden, three good meals a day, library, pool, clubhouse, security – everything you could wish for.

'After six months, I was beginning to relax and feel she'd at last settled down, and then I got a phone call telling me she'd stolen a pair of wire cutters from the residents' workshop and cut her way out. I was away on business at the time and she broke into my apartment, dug out her passport and personal documents and literally flew the coop, off again to God knows where.'

'You've got to hand it to her, old chap. She's always been a goer. How old would she be now?'

'Eighty-two,' mumbled Charles, obviously embarrassed.

'So what brings you to London?'

'Well,' said Aubrey, 'I happened to be reading a magazine in the urologist's ...'

'Yes, I always find it's better to have something to read while you're flashing your arse at the urologist,' said Charles. 'It makes one feel so vulnerable.'

'No, I was in the waiting room actually. I think it was a magazine called *Jet Set Seniors*. And there, staring out at me was a photo of my mother, strapped into a

18

parachute, wearing a blue sequined jumpsuit with matching helmet, holding a bottle of Champagne, and doing a tumble roll as she landed in Hyde Park! And they say she didn't spill a drop!'

Charles tried hard to suppress a giggle. 'She always knew how to hold her liquor.'

'I checked with the magazine editor and Immigration and it now appears she's flown out to Tierra del Fuego!'

Charles chuckled and said, 'Oh, let her go, Aubs. She's obviously doing what she wants to. '

'But she *needs* me!' expounded Aubrey. 'She's an old lady! I *have* to look after her.'

Charles laid his hand on Aubrey's arm. 'What does she need you for, to hold her hand while she scuba-dives the Antarctic? Let her be, Aubs, get on with your own life. What are you doing now, anyway, apart from hounding your poor, white-headed old mother?'

'I'm in real estate back in Australia. Surfers Paradise – you remember, on the Gold Coast, Queensland.'

'Right. Any good?' asked Charles.

'Not bad,' replied Aubrey, modestly. 'Well, actually I've done very well really. You should check it out sometime. Come for a holiday.'

'Oh, I'd love to personally, but I don't think I'd ever convince the Lady Celia to travel that far.'

'Lady Celia?' queried Aubrey.

'My wife,' explained Charles a little sullenly. 'Big woman – well, huge actually, daughter of Lord Swindon.'

Aubrey smiled. 'Aristocracy! Well, I am impressed – not surprised though, knowing you.'

'I was trapped, Aubs. I met her at a weekend hunt in the Cotswolds. She was only young, not what you'd call pretty – homely would be over exaggerated, and not fully developed then either. When we were introduced, she leant towards me and pushed her face at me. I presumed I was expected to give her one of those air-peck kisses on each cheek; you know that ridiculous social convention that women persist in practising at functions and parties, even if they hate each other. Well, I leaned forward to oblige and the next thing I knew she'd slid one hand behind my neck and, with a vice-like grip pulled me into a full-blown pash, sticking her tongue down my throat like a boa constrictor seeking refuge, while her other hand groped my balls. Her father, Lord Swindon, always looking for the chance of getting rid of his unattractive and embarrassing daughter, saw this as a sterling opportunity and announced to the rest of the gathering that his "little" Celia had obviously found her lifetime mate, which of course was taken almost as an official engagement announcement in those days.'

He paused, ruminating upon his mistake. 'With the offer of a large house in London, a sizeable dowry, a generous yearly allowance from Lord Swindon, and a position in one of his banks, what was I to do in my situation? I'm ashamed to say, and, as you know, so unlike me, I threw my principles to the wind and stepped into a tornado! We were married before the taste of her tongue down my throat had subsided. I sold myself, Aubs,' Charles said miserably, 'and lived to regret it.'

Aubrey smiled sympathetically. 'I take it there were no children?'

'Are you mad? The last time she asked me to climb on top of her, I got altitude sickness and frostbite on my arse. It was like climbing Everest without Sherpas or staging camps.'

At this point Charles' mobile phone started playing 'There'll Always Be an England' and he scrabbled around in his pockets trying to find it. 'Excuse me, Aubs,' and into the phone he said, 'Charles Wellington?' Obviously the caller was very distressed, rattling on and ignoring Charles' attempts to interrupt. 'Now calm down, Rodney – Just slow down and tell me exactly what happened.' He listened and gradually his face turned ashen. 'I see. Now don't panic. I'll get over there as soon as I can.' He disconnected the line and thoughtfully replaced the mobile back into his pocket.

Aubrey looked at him questioningly, 'Something wrong?'

Charles sighed and rose from the bar stool. 'Slight business problem.'

'Anything I can do to help?' asked Aubrey, also rising.

'I doubt it but come along and we'll drop in on the way back to your hotel,' replied Charles as they made their way to the exit.

The Rolls pulled up in a fashionable laneway in the East End. Aubrey was quite impressed with the Roller but Charles dismissed it as another perk from Lord Swindon to the Lady Celia. Not that she drove around in it herself because, as Charles explained, she couldn't fit behind the steering wheel and even getting her into the back passenger seat required greasing her body and the assistance of two strong men with crowbars. If she went out socially they hired a furniture van, he sniffed.

The gilt sign over the front entrance read 'Champagne Charlie's Hotel for Gentlemen'. Charles led Aubrey up a narrow staircase to the first floor of the building. It was an older Victorian design that had been renovated after bomb damage from the Second World War, but still had the overdone style of a faded bordello, with lots of faded red décor and gilt fittings. The door to the premises was splintered and ajar. They entered a small reception area that appeared to have been ransacked: mirrors smashed, holes punched in the walls, windows broken with shards of glass lying all over the place. A chandelier, barely hanging from its electrical cable, looked as though it was about to fall onto the slashed, red plush, velvet settee.

Charles stood in the middle of the room surveying the carnage, anxiously calling out, 'Rodney? ... Rodney?' There was no answer. He walked up a once-gilt-railed staircase to the next floor and along a corridor with several rooms opening off it, still calling out but to no avail. He returned to the reception area where Aubrey, still open mouthed, stood bewildered, as Charles moved to the reception desk

'My God, what a mess!' exclaimed Aubrey. 'Someone's really done it over. It looks like a cheap, ransacked brothel.'

'It is,' said Charles casually, reading a note he had picked up from the desk. 'Or rather, it was.'

Aubrey was astounded. 'You mean you actually own a brothel?'

'No, of course not,' scoffed Charles, affronted. 'Lord Swindon owns it, I just ran it.'

'You were a madam?' said Aubrey.

'No,' Charles retorted huffily, 'I managed it. Rodney was the madam. And God knows where he is now. According to his note, the Bray Brothers gang paid him another visit. This is the fourth time,' he said, glancing up at Aubrey with a worried look. 'Apparently they sliced him up a bit and threatened to come back and finish the job if the place opened again.' He indicated a couple of dried blood spots on the note as proof. 'They smashed the place up, rounded up the girls and took them away, and I guess this is Rodney's formal resignation.' Charles looked sadly defeated.

'Are you going to ring the police?' asked Aubrey.

'And report my brothel had been ransacked? I think not,' said Charles. 'There seem to be more immediate concerns. Read this.' He handed Aubrey the note.

'They've threatened you too, Charles,' said Aubrey astounded, reading the note. 'Oh my God! Could they actually train a greased rat to do that?'

'Oh yes,' replied Charles. 'Which would mean another visit to Peter Pointer, the proctologist, and I'm damned if I'm going to let him train a fox terrier to go up after it. Come on, let's get out of here. I think I'm suddenly out of the Gentlemen's Club business: Another corporate take-over.'

Chapter 3

Back at his hotel, Aubrey fretted about Charles. There was no doubt he'd mellowed a lot since they'd last known each other, and Aubrey felt immensely sad for his old school chum. Although there were remnants of the old Charles, his unhappy marriage, his unfortunate ties to his odious father-in-law, his desperate attempts to survive in a world of comfort and financial security, which it appeared was often on the edge of 'respectability' and on the borderline of the law, had obviously taken their toll. Otherwise why on earth would he possibly stay in real estate?

He determined that he would talk to Charles the next day and try to convince him to relocate to Australia where at least he could keep an eye on him and maybe help him to recover some of the *joi de vivre* of old. Aubrey was like that: always a softie and out to help an old friend in need of kindness and understanding. If he could convince Charles to immigrate, or even come for a working holiday, with Aubrey's contacts, he would be able to help him get work in Queensland. With Charles back to his old self, he may do very well on the Gold Coast. After all, many a Pom with true con-man instincts had made a fortune there in real estate.

He rang Charles at home early the next morning. The phone was answered by the redoubtable Lady Celia.

Her caged-wild-animal growl informed him that she had no idea of the whereabouts of her useless, philandering husband, but she had been led to believe that he usually took breakfast at a café in The Strand called The Joker, which she thought entirely appropriate. He thanked her before she could call her keeper and hurried down to the lobby and hailed a taxi.

As predicted, Aubrey found Charles sitting alone at a table, eating his croissant and drinking black coffee, while nervously checking out the passing traffic and pedestrians in fear of becoming the victim of a drive-by shooting, or a car bomb attack by the infamous Bray Brothers gang. Aubrey settled in the chair opposite Charles, who gave an involuntary start and removed his dark sunglasses.

'Mind if I join you?' Aubrey said as he picked up the menu. 'Lady Celia told me you'd probably be here.'

'You actually talked to her?' asked Charles. 'I thought she'd be in her cage being fed her breakfast bison at this hour.'

Aubrey smiled and looked out at the drizzling rain blowing in cold drafts down the street. 'You know, if we were on the Gold Coast, we'd be sitting at an outdoor café in the warm sun, eating crisp bacon and eggs, grilled tomatoes and toast, and watching the white foam capped, crystal-clear waves rolling onto the golden beach, and bronzed surfers riding their boards through the pipelines of the surf.'

'Humph,' said Charles. 'And waving our arms around to chase away the flies, and stomping our feet to scare

26

off the venomous snakes and spiders, while the kangaroos attacked the koalas at the next table, and the sharks chomped on a slow-swimming Japanese tourist in the shallows.'

Aubrey laughed. 'Well, it keeps the tourists down to manageable numbers.' He looked at his friend soulfully. 'Come back with me, Charles. It's just the change you need. I get the feeling the tide is running out for you here and there are still plenty of opportunities for a man like you over there. In fact, I've got a couple of business deals I think you could help me with. We're both in real estate, we're both still healthy and we're both still alive.'

'But for how long?' said Charles gloomily, contemplating his uncertain future with the Bray Brothers gang. 'Look at me, Aubs, I'm almost fifty.' Aubrey snorted. 'Well all right, pushing sixty,' confessed Charles. 'It's a young person's world. We're irrelevant, past our use-by date, and whether I like it or not, and I certainly don't, I'm stuck with "The Towering Glacier"' and the father-in-law from Hell, and they know it.

'The Gold Coast is full of ageing people,' said Aubrey, 'It's a retiree's dream. And a lot of those retirees have money. It's a wonderful life for the young and old. Come on, give it a try: even if it's just for a holiday – why not check it out?'

Charles looked at his friend for a long time, daring to consider that there may be an answer to his seemingly hopeless situation. Suddenly the old twinkle came back into his eye. 'They're not still transporting convicts to the Colonies, are they, Aubs?'

Aubrey shot him a worried look, 'You don't have a police record, do you, Charles?'

Charles laughed. 'Of course not, Aubs.'

Aubrey sighed in relief.

'They could never prove a thing.' Charles added.

'Well, in that case, Charles,' his friend smiled, 'I'm afraid you're going to have to pay your own way.'

Chapter 4

Charles walked into his office at Twilight Escorts, flopped into his revolving chair and spun around to face the window. His view was not of the beach and rolling surf, but of a plain brick wall. Well, the wall was plain the last time he looked at it but in the meantime a graffiti artist had dug deep into his creative genius and painted:

Uthanasia Shud'nt be a Choyce It Shud Be Obligatry

Charles scowled, and spun back in his chair mumbling, 'The ignorant little sod, can't even spell!' He reached for his intercom: 'Ms Twigden,' he growled, 'would you ask Gavin to clean the graffiti off the wall again, please?

'Yes, Mr Charles, I'll see to it right away. Oh, and Ms Therese Singleton is here for her appointment.'

Charles sighed, 'Send her in, Ms Twigden.'

Aubrey sat at his desk checking paperwork. There was a tap on the door and Estelle entered, carrying a cup and saucer with two home-made biscuits. 'Thought you might like a nice cuppa, Mr Aubrey. Mr Charles is interviewing Ms Singleton. Do you want to see her before she goes?'

'I don't think that will be necessary, Ms Twigden, Charles will buzz me if it is.'

'And Delilah-nee-Delma at number eleven wants the thermostat on her oven checked. She says she keeps burning her cakes.'

'Thank you, Ms Twigden, get Gavin to have a look at it when he's got a minute.'

'Probably using the fan forced setting instead of bake,' said Estelle. 'I keep telling her that fan forced is hotter than bake.'

'You're probably right,' said Aubrey. 'If she only knew as much about cooking as you do, Ms Twigden. These biscuits are wonderful.'

Estelle blushed. 'Thank you, Mr Aubrey. I've had a lot of practice, what with Mother being so fussy.'

'Oh, yes,' he said, remembering, 'how's she getting on at the Home? Still abusing the staff?

'I'm afraid so,' said Estelle sadly. 'She threw a commode pot at a nurse again the other day. Luckily it was only urine this time.'

'Yes, well, better than last time, I suppose,' said Aubrey. 'That time it *really* hit the fan, as they say.'

'Yes, I suppose so,' said Estelle. 'But her aim is improving.'

'Well, any improvement is a blessing,' said Aubrey.

'And what is your current marital situation, Ms Singleton?' Charles asked the applicant sitting opposite.

'Married, widowed, married, divorced, widowed, not married, single, and available,' said Therese, ticking the order off on her fingers.

Therese was an expensively, and unsuitably, over-dressed woman that Charles judged to be in her early sixties. She'd obviously had a lot of 'corrective' surgery, but correction had not been enough. What she really needed was a complete re-construction. In fact, Charles was of the opinion that she'd had so many face-lifts, if she hadn't shaved, she would've been sporting a Tasmania-shaped goatee. The skin on her face was tanned and leathery and so tight you could bounce a twenty-cent piece off it. If she could puff her cheeks out, they would've made an excellent drum kit for a rock band.

Charles also noted she had forgotten to have the skin of her upper arms removed, and at first he'd thought she was wearing a long-sleeved blouse. Charles summed her up as being just a little 'coarse'.

'And it says here on your application form you are forty-seven?' he said, trying to keep the utter disbelief from his voice.

'Yeah, that's right,' said Therese, without a flicker of hesitation, but with a slight twitch in her left eye that gave her away.

'And your photograph,' he said picking up the ten-by-eight lying in front of him, 'Do you have anything more recent? The beehive hairstyle doesn't really do you justice.'

'I think it makes me look taller.'

'And the bikini ...'

'That was an original Paula Stafford,' she interrupted proudly, referring to the famous Australian designer of the fifties and sixties.

'Yes, but it's not quite the image we like to project. The python is very nice though. Might be able to get him some work,' Charles joked with a forced laugh.

'He's dead now,' Therese replied with a straight face. 'That was Bobby. I used to do an act with him and my partner, Neville. He was a jealous bastard.'

'Neville?'

'No, Bobby. He thought Neville used to get into more interesting places than he did.' She laughed uproariously.

'Right. You see,' he said, changing the subject tactfully, 'our agency only deals with escorts in the over-fifty age bracket. There are enough agencies around to cater for the younger people, but there are a lot of lonely old – I mean mature, independent, single men and women out there who are desperate for a bit of companionship now that their partners have – moved on, for one reason or another. Our agency gives them the opportunity to continue an enjoyable social life with suitable partners of a similar age, for any occasion that may present itself: parties, theatre or movies, dining, fishing, bushwalking or picnics even; anywhere they would like to go with someone for company, with no commitment or strings attached. And why shouldn't they? There's no reason why they should sit at home by themselves, reading, watching television, or knitting, when there is so much life and enjoyment available out there waiting for them.'

'Sounds right up my alley,' said Therese. 'I love a bit of fun meself. What's the pay like?'

'The client is charged a reasonable fee and we deduct a commission and expenses. The rest goes to the escort. It works very well.' He paused, thinking how to frame the words for his next comment. 'Now, unfortunately, at the age you've given me, you fall into the too-young bracket for our requirements for an escort,' he smiled as though disappointed, 'so I'm afraid, Therese, under our strict guidelines, we wouldn't be in a position to offer you any work.'

There was a pause while Therese let it sink in, and then she looked up shrewdly at Charles and, again with the slight twitch in her left eye, she said, 'How about sex?'

Charles smiled a little patronisingly and said, 'No, I thought I'd explained, we do not encourage our escorts or clients to indulge in anything but companionship.'

'I'm not talking about them,' said Therese, 'I mean you and me. Would that help me to get the job?

Chapter 5

Aubrey had been thrilled when Charles rang him from London, saying he'd decided to take him up on his suggestion and come out to Australia for a trip. On principle, Charles had extended an invitation, albeit half-heartedly, to the Lady Celia to join him but thankfully she'd declined, saying, 'Are you a complete idiot? Orstralia? It's on the other side of the planet! It's filled with cricketers and all those other awful sports people. I'd rather die!' which Charles thought an excellent alternative. However, he did offer to charter a large container ship for her if she changed her mind, a cargo plane being out of the question.

Aubrey had met Charles at the airport and driven him back to Surfers Paradise giving him a short tour on the way. Charles was absolutely amazed at the scenery, the beautiful clear, blue sky and the wonderful warm sun. The long stretches of clean beaches, the incredible aqua blue water, and high-rise apartment buildings, delighted and intrigued him. There were many tourists of course, but there was such a relaxed feeling to the place, it felt immediately exhilarating.

They stopped for coffee at a popular beachside café. A mix of nationalities sat at the other tables, but the patrons were predominately white, Charles was amazed to note. He sat back in his chair and relaxed taking in the ambience, while Aubrey ordered their drinks.

'Well, what do you think?' asked Aubrey, as he settled in a chair opposite.

'Bloody marvellous,' replied Charles. 'I never realised it would be so – sophisticated. I can see what you mean about retirees,' he said looking around the other patrons. 'But they all look so much younger than the ones back home: tanned, and they dress so well.'

'There's a lot of money on this stretch,' said Aubrey. 'The houses and apartments sell for millions of dollars.'

Charles whistled appreciatively. 'I can understand why,' he said. 'It beats a lot of the over-populated spots on the Continent. And it's all so clean and new looking.'

'Now, I've put you up in an apartment block I own,' said Aubrey. 'I think you'll be comfortable there. Two bedrooms, bathroom, kitchen, sitting room with a balcony, not much of a view I'm afraid.'

'Sounds perfect,' said Charles, 'but just a room would've done, old man.'

'Nonsense,' said Aubrey. 'Besides, I have an ulterior motive. I've only just bought the block and I'd like your ideas about the possibilities. It's a bit ordinary by today's standards.'

'Well remember, I'm only a "new chum", I think you call it. I'd like to get the lie of the land before I'd dare to make any suggestions.'

'Take as long as you like,' said Aubrey.

That was almost three years ago and Aubrey and Charles had now reaffirmed their former close, boyhood friendship; Aubrey because he hadn't formed many friendships and those he had were mostly connected to business, and Charles, suddenly released from the Lady Celia, his dominating father-in-law and his somewhat shady past, had blossomed into a more relaxed and happy person who had kept deferring his return to the Home Country, and extending his tourist visa. Business had flourished, in a large part due to Charles' craftiness and flair for original ideas, which had been denied him during his long and restrictive married life.

He had moved into the apartment and settled into the lifestyle relatively quickly. Unlike his prior life, he was up and awake quite early every morning, exploring the neighbourhood at first, and then later, hiring a car and going further afield, driving around and absorbing the entire coastal and hinterland strip. He read the daily newspapers and watched the news and documentaries on television avidly. He nearly always lunched with Aubrey and at weekends they would spend time visiting areas and tourist spots that Aubrey had never appreciated before. As a newcomer, Charles saw things in a different light and soon the germ of an idea was forming in his opportunistic brain.

One evening at dinner when they were both feeling relaxed and mellow after a delicious seafood meal and a couple of bottles of excellent Australian chardonnay, Charles was finally ready to broach the subject that, by then, had become so dear to his heart.

36

'Aubs,' he said, 'when I arrived on the Coast you said you were after ideas for the apartment block I'm living in.'

'Mmm,' said Aubrey, 'and what have you come up with?'

'Well,' said Charles, 'first of all, as you said, those apartments are a little out of date, and the building doesn't really lend itself to up-market, luxury living. I mean, it's quite central but there's no ocean view of course. And I've been thinking about the number of retirees either living here or, more importantly, moving here.'

'So?' said Aubrey.

'Well, did you know there are over fifteen hundred people a week moving up to Queensland?'

'I am in real estate remember, Charles.'

'And a lot of those are older people from a constantly ageing population, right?' continued Charles.

Aubrey nodded and took another sip of wine.

'Now there are a lot of over-fifties developments on the Coast: retirement villages, over-fifties resorts and so on. I think there could be a demand for the over fifties who don't feel they're ready yet for a retirement village. And maybe they'd prefer to rent rather than buy, and free up some of their capital. Maybe some of them want to live in, say, a block of apartments with similar facilities to some of the ones I've seen, without actually moving into a retirement home as such. Yours hasn't got the view but with a little alteration and a few improvements, I think your block would be admirable. They'd be close to

37

the action and, with an age group restriction, they'd feel more secure and not have to put up with young, maybe noisy tourists, or young families, and still be able to form a community without the "Old Age" label. The Baby Boomers don't want to be thought of as old. They still think of themselves as the swingers of the seventies.'

'Don't we all,' smiled Aubrey, aiming his remark at Charles who completely ignored it.

'What do you think?' asked Charles.

'Well, I agree about the Baby Boomer market. A lot of them spent up big and went into debt, and when it came to retirement, they suddenly found they didn't have enough put by to live in the style they were accustomed to. They sold their lavish houses and by the time they paid off the huge mortgages and debts, there was precious little left to buy something smaller and have enough to live on for the rest of their lives. The rental market could be a key.'

He considered the proposal as he poured wine into each of their glasses. 'How much would these "alterations and improvements" cost, do you think?' asked Aubrey.

Charles shrugged. 'Haven't done the figures precisely,' he said, 'but I'd be more than willing to contribute a share if you were interested.'

'A partnership?' asked Aubrey.

'Why not?' said Charles.

'But aren't you planning to return to the Lady Celia?'

'Good God, why? Anyway, I don't think she's even realised I've gone.'

'You did tell her you were coming over here, didn't you?'

'Of course I told her. I actually invited her to join me but she absolutely refused, thank God. Then I left a couple of weeks later and wrote her a letter on the plane saying I was on my way. I posted it the moment I arrived in Australia.'

'You mean you didn't actually say goodbye to her?'

'You mean, face to face? Are you mad? She and her bloody father would've had me strapped to her scratching pole and fed on her gazelle leftovers. No, a nice chatty letter was much better, and safer.'

Aubrey shook his head in amazement.

'Well, are we partners or not?' urged Charles.

Aubrey smiled. 'I'll think about it,' he said as he extended his hand, 'depending on the costing.'

'Oh, don't worry about that, Aubs, if the worst comes to the worst, I'll cut Lord Swindon in on the deal.'

Under the circumstances, Aubrey had his doubts on that score.

'Oh, and there's one more thing,' said Charles. 'I have another idea. It's sort of related to the apartment deal.'

Aubrey looked at him with interest.

'You know the front apartment; the one on the ground floor that faces the street?'

Aubrey nodded.

'Well, that would make an ideal office.'

'For the reception, you mean?' said Aubrey. 'Would we need one that big?'

'Not for the apartments,' said Charles. 'For the escort agency.'

Aubrey almost bit a chunk out of his wine glass. 'Escort agency?'

'Yes,' said Charles, 'I have this super idea to open an escort agency for the over fifties.'

'A brothel?' Aubrey shouted, in horrified disbelief. 'You want to open a geriatric knock shop?'

The woman at the next table choked on her bouillabaisse and had to be escorted to the Ladies' Room. Charles gestured for Aubrey to keep his voice down.

'No, no, not a knock shop – an escort agency,' Charles whispered.

'And I suppose you want to install a Viagra dispenser in the foyer?' an outraged Aubrey almost shouted.

Charles' eyes lit up. 'What a super idea! I've got a marvellous supplier in India I found on the web, very cheap.'

'Charles,' said Aubrey in a warning voice.

'No, I'm kidding,' Charles chuckled, 'a proper and respectable escort agency. I got the idea when I found out how many single or unattached oldies visited or lived on the coast. And the number of conventions they hold up here. Just think of it. There must be hundreds of older folk who would appreciate being able to hire an escort for the night – or day,' he added quickly. 'You know, to accompany them out to formals, or dinner, or outings, or anything; just for company. Sex wouldn't come into it. Well, if it did it would have nothing to do

40

with the agency. We'd be a thoroughly "respectable" establishment dealing in "respectable" companionship.'

Aubrey studied his beaming, excited face. 'You're serious.'

'Entirely,' said Charles.

Aubrey's mind went into over-drive, daring to even consider such an outrageous idea.

Chapter 6

Charles met Penny on his very first excursion to the beach. He arrived all prepared as he would have in Brighton; his only concession to Australian beachwear attire being a pair of pale green baggy shorts, too long or too short to be fashionable, a cream, open-necked shirt with long sleeves, a crumpled towelling hat that he'd shoved in the glove-box of the car, and to complete the ensemble, calf-length, tan-coloured golf socks, worn under a pair of brown leather open sandals. He carried a collapsible green-striped deckchair, a small beach bag, and a new beach towel emblazoned with a pattern of the English flag.

Of course he did not intend to actually go in swimming. He had a paralysing fear of sharks, or even sardines, if it came to that. He just wanted to sit on the beach, soak up the sun and absorb the atmosphere. He chose his spot with a good view of the beach-goers frolicking in the waves, surfers displaying amazing agility on their surfboards, and the mostly young, gorgeous, tanned, healthy-looking bodies. He removed a paperback detective story from his bag in case he got bored with the view, which was very unlikely under the circumstances, sat back and relaxed.

A bright voice next to him with a cockney accent suddenly said, 'Oi, I bet you're a Pom.'

He turned to look at the owner of the voice and, squinting from the sun, saw a beautiful, slim, blonde-headed young lady with a streak of bright blue in her wet head-clinging hair.

'I am English, if that's what you mean. How did you guess?'

Penny laughed and introduced herself. 'I'm from the Old Country meself; takes one to know one. My name's Penny. Just arrived out here, have you?'

'Well yes, as a matter of fact, another good guess.'

Penny laughed again. 'Not really. I can tell the signs. I'd put some suntan cream on my face if I were you. The sun gets pretty fierce. Mind you, up here the weather doesn't change all that much. You'll know it's summer when you burn your hands on the steering wheel.'

'But I've got a hat on, and my arms and legs are covered.'

'Yeah, but still, it's best to be on the safe side. Here, I'll put some of mine on ya.' She tipped some lotion on her hand and gently applied it to his cheeks and forehead. 'What's ya name?'

'Charles, Charles Wentworth, I've just arrived out from London.'

'I've got an uncle lives in London: Uncle George, haven't seen him since I was a kid. I've been out here for years, since I was sixteen,' Penny said. 'I'm a True Blue Aussie now.'

There was no doubt Penny was an attractive girl, no matter what colour. 'I'm just out on a hol,' said Charles.

'Well, in that case, I think it's my duty to educate you a bit in the way of Aussie-dom.' She settled herself down next to him on the sand. 'Now pay attention otherwise you'll be treated as a foreigner. First of all, the L in the word Australia is optional and the word should be pronounced "Astraya"; the plural for "you" is always "youse", the "girt by sea" in the national anthem has nothing to do with Gertrude sitting by the water, and Aussies get choked up with the first verse of their national anthem and can't remember the words of the second verse. Stubbies can be either worn or drunk, Kylie Minogue is known as the girl from *Neighbours*, and never ask anyone for a rubber if you want an eraser.'

Charles laughed uncertainly, not quite understanding what she was talking about.

'And let me see,' she said, racking her brain, 'oh, and the black axle grease they put on their toast is called Vegemite, and must be avoided at all costs. A group of girls wearing "thongs" may not be as attractive as it sounds because they're actually wearing flip flops, and during the drought, you may as well turn your garden hose into a bong rather than get prosecuted for watering your garden.'

Charles laughed even louder and said, 'I thought it was bad enough being brutally strip-searched by the customs officers in case I was trying to sneak in an apple or an orange.'

'Oh yeah,' she said, 'you might get away with a few drugs, but fruit and vegetables and anything made of wood are a big no-no.'

They both laughed uproariously then Penny stood up and said, 'Come on, take off your shirt, socks and sandals and we'll go for a paddle in the water.'

Charles was reluctant. 'What about the sharks?'

Penny laughed. 'The only white pointers you'll have to worry about will be walking around in bikinis.' She held out her hand to help him up. 'Come on.'

As they walked along the beach, ankle deep in the crystal-clear water, there was suddenly a commotion, with groups of people shouting and pointing out to sea. Charles immediately thought there must've been a shark attack but Penny laughed and reassured him, indicating a large black hump rising out of the water, hundreds of metres from the shore. 'Look, it's a whale,' she cried excitedly.

Charles studied it carefully for a while and said, 'Thank God for that. I thought the Lady Celia had made up her mind to join me after all, and decided to swim out.'

That night while Charles and Aubrey were dining, Charles regaled Aubrey with tales of his exciting day. 'And I was amazed at the extraordinarily well-endowed young men in those skimpy swimmers. Pee-cock Pouches I think Penny called them.'

Aubrey thought for a moment and chuckled. 'I think you mean Budgie Smugglers.'

'Oh, right,' said Charles, standing corrected. 'Budgie Smugglers.'

By the time Charles went to bed that night he could hardly move. He'd forgotten to apply the sunscreen lotion to his back after he'd taken off his shirt. He'd learned his lesson, and from that day on he never left the apartment without sun protection.

On his next excursion to the beach he arrived looking much more casual. He'd daringly decided to adopt the Budgie Smuggler look but, feeling a little self-conscious, he'd rolled up his golf socks and shoved them down the front of his newly acquired Lycra swimmers to enhance his 'manhood'. His Budgie Smugglers turned out looking more like a 'Vulture Vehicle' and drew much attention and, in some cases, envy. Unfortunately, while he was walking along the water's edge, a large dumper wave crashed onto the beach, thoroughly drenching him. When it receded, he was sopping wet from head to toe and the tan golf socks had dislodged themselves and finished up between the cheeks of his bum. And worse still, the socks had unravelled a bit and the toe of one of them escaped through the leg hole of his trunks and was hanging down his leg. 'Ooh, look, Mummy,' said a small child nearby. 'That old man's shit himself!'

Chapter 7

Over the following weeks, Charles and Penny met regularly at the beach and enjoyed each other's company enormously. Penny also introduced him to the 'club scene' and they spent many a happy time 'bopping to the beat' as Charles called it, and getting very drunk on rum and Coke.

In the meantime, plans went ahead fairly smoothly with the apartment alterations and Charles was like a kid with a new toy. Aubrey still wasn't convinced about the suitability or viability of the escort agency idea but it got to the stage where he had to make a decision. Influenced by Charles' excitement, he finally gave in and acquiesced to his plan, saying as long as it was kept scrupulously 'respectable,' he would go along with it. After all, he thought, if it didn't work out, they could always convert the office back into an apartment.

They had decided on the terms and infrastructure of the venture, with Charles and Aubrey as full partners, sharing the duties and responsibilities. Although Charles was now a partner and close friend, Aubrey knew his friend of old and thought it best to stay as fully involved as possible to keep an eye on proceedings. To facilitate this, Aubrey decided to move his permanent office to the escort agency.

Eventually the project was finished and Charles excitedly took Aubrey on a tour of the completed premises, pointing out their individual offices, the front reception with its desks, computers, filing cabinets and other smart but tasteful office equipment. The one- and two-bedroom apartments had been completely refurbished and air conditioned, and more glass had been added for extra light and space; balconies had been extended to make room for outside dining furniture and a pot plant garden, and the original pool had been solar heated with attractive gazebos dotted around the tile surrounds and gardens, for shade. All in all, it was very comfortable for the requirements of aging tenants.

Inspecting the garden, Aubrey stopped at a modern-looking sculpture. 'What's that?'

Charles giggled almost boyishly and said, 'It's a sculpture – made entirely of solar panels! Isn't it marvellous? Cheap power.'

'Well, it's certainly – different,' conceded Aubrey, eyeing the structure dubiously.

Later, they discussed plans for advertising and promotion. Aubrey came up with the idea that the apartments should be called 'Autumn Twilight Apartments', and Charles agreed. 'That's very suitable, Aubs, and we could call the escort business "The Twilight Escort Agency". You get it – T.E.A., tea?'

'Right. And maybe a good slogan would be "TEA and Sympathy",' suggested Aubrey, stealing the name of a famous play from the fifties.

'Or "TEA and Crumpet",' suggested Charles.

Aubrey gave him a warning scowl and Charles raised his hands placatingly saying, 'All right, all right, sorry.'

The advertisements were placed and the date for interviewing intended applicants was set. That was how Estelle entered the picture. She was already working for Aubrey in his real estate office and, aware of her loyalty and professional work ethic, he approached her with an offer to join him and Charles in the new venture, to be in charge of the office administration. Surprisingly she jumped at the chance and thought both ventures would be hugely successful. Her attitude toward the escort agency was an even bigger surprise, as being an apparently very conservative person, he had imagined, wrongly as it turned out, that she would be horrified. If anything, her attitude even encouraged Aubrey into feeling that maybe Charles' idea wasn't as outrageous as he had thought.

Unfortunately, Aubrey had hired Estelle without prior discussion with Charles on the subject of staff, so Charles was a little disappointed and frankly horrified, especially when he actually came face to face with their new Office Manager, who was not exactly the type Charles had in mind. It was the first real disagreement they had.

'She looks like a possible customer for the escort agency,' complained Charles later. 'She looks so ...' he searched for a suitable word, 'dried up – like the centrefold of the *Embalmer's Weekly*. I wouldn't say she was ugly but if she went to a beauty parlour it would take two hours just for an estimate. She may not be old but she's certainly chronologically challenged.'

'She'll be marvellous,' Aubrey assured him. 'She's excellent with figures.'

'Well, she hasn't done so well with her own,' Charles retorted.

'And she is excellent at multi-tasking,' Aubrey extolled.

'And what does that mean – she can laugh, cough, sneeze, fart and pee, all at the same time?'

'Just give her a chance, Charles. I'm sure you'll be surprised.'

'I'll be surprised if she doesn't scare away the applicants,' said Charles. 'What did you say her name was?'

'Estelle Twigden,' said Aubrey, patiently.

'ET?' Charles nodded. 'How appropriate. Aubs, I suggest we both interview any further staff, and the applicants for tenancy, from now on. We have to look outside the box and when I say, outside the box, I don't mean a coffin.'

'Very well, Charles, but may I remind you, we are now dealing with mature, ageing personalities, and not customers and staff for your common knock shop in Soho. Estelle is just the sort of manager they will be able to empathise with and relate to.'

'It wasn't a common knock shop,' retorted Charles, outraged. 'It was a Gentlemen's Club.'

'A brothel by any other name, Charles, is still a knock shop.'

Chapter 8

The day of the interviews arrived and Estelle, true to form, arrived early to organise the various forms and clipboards. She was amazed and gratified to see how many applicants were there already. Aubrey and Charles had decided to hold the interviews for both the apartment rentals, and applicants for escorts, on the same day, thinking they may find some applicants suitable for both.

This was actually Charles' idea. 'If we get people suitable for the apartment rental, as well as escorts, it would be an advantage, as we can keep an eye on both aspects at the same time. Maybe we can offer a rent discount for anybody who wants to join the agency as well. That way, they'd be close at hand when we wanted them.'

Aubrey was dubious. He didn't really expect many to turn up for the escort work, and wasn't entirely happy about all the escorts living in the same place, in case it gave the agency the image of a bordello, which was to be avoided at all costs. However, he was prepared to consider the idea. But he insisted it shouldn't be a prerequisite.

Charles arrived late of course, claiming the alarm clock hadn't gone off, but Aubrey reminded him that he had tried to wake him several times but Charles had been too hung-over from the previous night's clubbing. So Aubrey arrived first with Charles assuring him he would follow as soon as he had showered and dressed. Consequently, by the time Charles arrived, there was an even bigger group of elderly people queued up outside the office and stretching down the street. As he went to enter the premises, there were a couple of shouts for him to 'Get in line, mate!' and 'Hey, no queue jumping.'

He waved aside the tactless insults and entered the office to find Estelle flat out, trying to cope with the numbers. 'Morning ET – my God, what a turnout; it looks like pension day at the Post Office out there – or a line-up for the Salvation Army soup kitchen.'

'Cheeky bastard,' said one elderly gent, and another woman said, 'Bloody Poms. What's he talking about anyway, he looks old enough to have come out as a cabin boy on the First Fleet.'

Another woman said, 'Well, he should do well as an escort. I'd be tempted to cough up a few bucks for that body.'

Estelle ignored the remarks and said, 'Good morning, Mr Charles. Mr Aubrey is in his office. He's already started,' she said rather pointedly.

'Right,' said Charles brightly. 'I'll just pop my head in and let him know the relief has arrived from Mafeking.'

He gave a short knock on the door, opened it and entered Aubrey's office, which he again registered, with a little chagrin, had a better view than his. 'Morning, Aubs,' he said, immediately noting that Aubrey already had an applicant sitting opposite him. 'Oops, sorry,' he said.

'Oh, that's all right, Charles, this is Mrs Longville,' said Aubrey. 'You might like to have a word with her after we're finished. She's interested in renting an apartment and going on our books as an escort.'

'Well, how do you do, Mrs Longville,' smiled Charles charmingly, coming around the desk and offering his hand. He was pleasantly surprised to notice a very attractive-looking lady, possibly in her early fifties, tastefully and smartly dressed, smiling at him.

'Good morning,' she replied accepting his hand graciously. 'You must be Mr Wellington: Aubrey mentioned your name. I actually noticed you on the viewing day when I was inspecting the apartments. They're very nice.'

They'd held a viewing day for the apartments a week earlier and had been swamped with prospective tenants, but Aubrey and Charles had insisted on interviews to choose the successful tenants.

'I actually know Mrs Longville, Charles. Well, I know her through her late husband really. He was my bank manager.'

'Yes, he passed away three years ago,' said Mrs Longville. 'Our house is on the market. Aubrey's handling the sale, you see. It's far too large for me now and I was looking to downsize. We didn't have any children or grandchildren. Ewan, my late husband, managed other people's money far better than he managed ours unfortunately, and he was also a gambler, so when he passed away, I suddenly discovered there was very little left, and quite a few debts to clear as well, so renting an apartment like yours seemed ideal.'

'And the escort work?' asked Charles.

'I don't see why not,' she said. 'It sounds rather fun, as long as it's safe – and discreet.'

'Oh, quite,' said Charles. 'We'll be carefully vetting any prospective clients, I can assure you. And we'll even be giving our escorts nom de plumes if they wish to ensure their privacy.'

'That sounds most suitable,' said Mrs Longville. 'Shall I see you after I've finished with Aubrey?'

'Please do,' said Charles. He walked to the door, turned to Aubrey, and behind Mrs Longville's back, gave him a huge grin and a double thumbs-up sign, and disappeared through the door.

Out in Reception Charles was delighted to see Penny standing at the counter opposite a rather disapproving Estelle.

'Penny!' Charles exclaimed happily.

''Allo, Charlie,' replied Penny with a winning smile. 'There seems to be a bit of a mix-up.'

'Miss Pryce here tells me you have hired her to assist in the office,' Estelle said icily.

'Yes, that's right, Estelle. It certainly looks like I did the right thing, doesn't it? She'll be a marvellous help.'

'I do wish you had at least discussed it with me before you made a decision, Mr Charles. Is Mr Aubrey aware of this development?'

'Well, he will be now, won't he?' Charles said brightly. 'Penny's a – er – a niece of mine from England. Lovely girl, very bright. You two will get along fine together, I'm sure.'

Turning to Penny, he said, 'Righto, Penny, get cracking. Ms Twigden will show you the ropes,' and without waiting for the retort that was forming on Estelle's thin lips, he escaped into his office calling, 'You can show my next appointment in, Estelle.'

Estelle turned disapprovingly to Penny who returned her look with a beaming smile.

'Well, if that's the sort they're looking for as escorts,' said a very plain-looking, middle-aged woman sizing Penny up and down, to the lady sitting next to her shelling peas, 'I'm off,' and with that, she put her knitting away in a large handbag and stalked from the office.

Another buxom woman of indeterminate age, whose name was Beryl, was chatting to another lady waiting next to her. 'Oh, yes, I've done a lot of escort work. I used to work for a security company; you know, banks, payrolls, department stores, nightclubs, football matches.'

'I don't think that's quite the sort of escort work they're advertising for,' said the other lady pleasantly.

'Doesn't matter,' said the first lady, 'one escort job is pretty much the same as the next. I'm even licensed to carry a firearm.'

'Oh, really?' said the second lady. 'How nice for you.'

Charles sat at his desk interviewing a male applicant.

'Well, ya see, I never actually married. I was a roo shooter in the Northern Territory for most of me life. And to be honest with ya, I could never bring meself to actually commit to one woman. Oh, I liked 'em well enough, even the black ones, but marriage? No, not for me. Knock 'em an' nick off, was my motto. Besides, the roo shooting an' croc hunting had me away from civilisation for long stretches at a time, hence the black sheilas.'

'And so you're interested in the agency work, I gather?' said Charles, unobtrusively sizing the man up.

His name was Alec and Charles could see why he would have had success with the women in his earlier years. He was very tall with rugged features, extremely broad shouldered with a dark, sun-tanned skin.

Even at his age, which Alec had told him was sixty, he was still a very good-looking man, with blue eyes and attractive features, dark brown hair, maybe slightly thinning on top, but with a sprinkling of grey at the temples, which gave him an odd suave quality. He still wore his battered slouch hat and was dressed in khaki, which gave him the look of a strong, adventurous, big-game hunter, or an African safari leader. To his credit, he had removed the hat when he entered the office, which gave Charles a sign that he did at least have some social graces.

'Well, as I said, I've just moved down from the Territory an' I've been stayin' in a flea-pit lodgin' 'ouse down the coast a bit an' I reckon it's time to move inta somethin' a bit more my style. I saw the apartments an'

56

thought one'd be beaut for me. So, if there's still one available, I'd like ta give it a go.'

'So, I take it you're interested in both of the offers we advertised?'

'If that's all right with you – yeah.'

Charles hesitated before saying, 'If we did decide to take you on the books as an escort, would you be prepared to agree to a couple of terms?'

'All depends,' said Alec, with just the edge of suspicion in his voice. 'Like what, fr'instance?'

'Well, there'd be the usual tenancy agreement for the apartment, and –' Charles tried to choose his words carefully so as not to offend or get a punch in the jaw, '– and how about some escort training?'

'Like what?' Alec said, wondering what on earth sort of training he could possibly need to be able to escort a lady out. He'd never had any complaints so far.

'Oh, maybe a few hints on dressing appropriately for an occasion, some speech lessons, perhaps?'

'What's wrong with the way I talk?' he asked, mystified.

'Nothing!' Charles reassured him urgently. 'Well, maybe your speech is just a little rough around the edges. It wouldn't take much, and I'm sure we could probably get you a lot of work if we just smoothed those edges out – just a little,' he added quickly. 'I think you could appeal to an even wider range of ladies.'

Alec thought about it for a minute and then said, 'If I have ta dress different, would I have ta wear underpants?'

That put Charles on the spot. 'Well, I don't suppose so. I mean, with a bit of luck, the ladies shouldn't notice, should they?'

'I wouldn't bet on that,' Alec replied with a wink. 'Look, I'm an ordinary sorta bloke an' I don't think I could stand too much variety in me women. I wouldn't want to disappoint 'em.' He gave the matter serious thought. 'But hey, why not? You're only old once, eh? Okay, sure,' he said making up his mind. 'Count me in.' Charles winced at the strength of Alex's handshake, imagining Alex wrestling a crocodile single handedly.

The interviews lasted well into the afternoon, by which time Aubrey, Charles, Estelle and Penny were becoming exhausted. The waiting line had now thankfully dwindled but there were still a few hopefuls left to interview. Charles came out of his office escorting his latest applicant and noted the remaining crowd, including a couple who had dropped off to sleep for their afternoon Nana Nap.

'Estelle,' he whispered, 'it's getting a bit late so, to save us a bit of time, why don't you take the gentlemen who are waiting into the back room and do a sort of pre-interview with them. I think we've decided on the suitable tenants for the apartments, so we just have to check out the likely escorts.'

'Well, I don't know, Mr Charles,' she whispered back. 'I'm not quite sure I'd know exactly what you are looking for.'

'You're a woman, Estelle, surely you can tell what sort of man a woman would like as an escort. If they don't come up to scratch, take their names and phone numbers and tell them we'll be in touch later.' He turned to the waiting crowd and raising his voice he said, 'Ladies and gentlemen, thank you for being so patient and we don't want to hold you up any longer than necessary, so if all the gentlemen who are interested in escort work will go with Ms Twigden here into the back room, she'll take down your particulars and we'll decide who will be the most suitable applicants. The successful ones will be asked to remain and wait for a further interview, the rest will be contacted later.'

There was a murmur of dissatisfaction from a few, but the men all stood with some reclaiming their walking sticks, and began to make their way to the back room, followed by Estelle, who said to Charles as she passed, 'I've never done this sort of thing before, Mr Charles, is there anything in particular you're looking for?'

'Oh, you know, Estelle, appearance, charm, manners, sex appeal.' As an afterthought he threw in jokingly, 'Check their rogers and make sure they're clean.'

Luckily Estelle didn't give the appearance of even hearing him as she traipsed after the men, with a studious, conscientious frown on her face.

Aubrey was interviewing a medium-height, rather good-looking and well-built Maori in his mid-fifties. 'And are you a permanent resident in Australia, Mr Kopa?'

'Yeh, of course, bro. Well, for the time bein' inyway. It depinds on me musses an' kuds beck home in New Ziland.'

'But would she mind you doing escort work?'

'Oh shit yeh, bro, she would'n mind. She's pretty staunch, eh. She's used to me playin' around wid other wimin. An' if it's makin' more money for us, even better.'

'You do understand, we're not asking you to prostitute yourself.'

' Ah …What's thet, bro?

'The work only requires you to escort ladies out on social occasions,' Aubrey explained. 'No sex is required.'

'No sux?'

'Pardon?'

'Sux, bro.'

'No, that's not required either: just company.'

'Don' know 'bout dat, bro, it's okay wi' me, but mos' wimin won' take no for an answer.'

'Well, I suggest you don't ask the question, Mr Kopa.'

Charles wrote *Doubtful, but may suit Kiwi women* on Mr Kopa's form and said, 'Well, thank you for coming in, Mr Kopa, we'll be in touch when we've decided.'

'Righto – ketch you lata, bro,' said Mr Kopa as he stood to leave.'

Charles and Aubrey met in the reception in between interviews.

'Going well, old man,' said Charles.

'Yes, surprisingly well,' said Aubrey. 'I must say I had my doubts about the escort agency idea, but I'm amazed at the turn-out, and the quality. Well, there have been quite a few unlikelies but that was only to be expected. A brilliant idea, Charles, and we'll have no trouble filling the apartments either.'

'Well, you just have to have a grasp on human nature, Aubs,' said Charles modestly, looking around the now almost deserted reception. 'Let's see how Estelle's been making out in the back room.'

'I don't think "making out" is the right phrase for Estelle, Charles,' said Aubrey chuckling.

They opened the door and walked in. Both Aubrey and Charles stopped dead in their tracks, Charles in amazement and Aubrey in shock, at the sight they beheld.

There, lined up in a row, were the six men Estelle had taken into the room to 'check out'. The men were standing entirely naked, apart from a couple wearing socks, and Estelle, with a tape measure around her neck, and a pad and pencil on the table in front of her, was saying, 'Thank you, gentlemen, you have been most obliging. You can all get dressed now and return to the reception, except –' checking her notes '– Mr Brewster and Mr Pemberton. We'll keep you on file and be in touch with you as required. Thank you all, again.'

The men started to dress and one of the old blokes said to another, 'Well, that's the funniest interview I've ever had. It was like having a check-up at the doctor's.'

'Well, I suppose they need to know if we're medically fit,' replied the other man.

Estelle came up to the still open-mouthed Charles and Aubrey with a satisfied smile. 'Well, that wasn't too bad,' she said. 'Four good ones and two who didn't quite measure up.' She passed them and walked back to her desk in reception.

Charles, with a sudden new-found respect for Estelle, and with a surprised but delighted smile, turned to Aubrey, exclaiming in a quasi-American accent, 'Right on, ET!'

Chapter 9

To celebrate the day's success, and to reward them for their hard work, Aubrey invited Charles, Penny and Estelle to dinner that night. They met at the restaurant and Penny arrived wearing a lovely purple dress that did marvels for her figure. Even her hair looked almost normal by her standards: swept up on the top of her head, and held by a purple and white artificial flower, which drew your attention away slightly from the blue streak.

Charles looked very dapper in a pale grey suit, with a darker grey silk shirt and a grey-and-white patterned tie, which for him was rather conservative. Aubrey, of course, wore a dark navy suit, white shirt, and maroon-and-blue striped tie and managed to look just like a real estate agent, out dining with clients.

They settled at the table Aubrey had booked, and waited for Estelle. Charles ordered a bottle of Piper-Heidsieck Champagne, which raised Aubrey's eyebrows somewhat as the most expensive champagne he had ever run to was a bottle of Great Western, and that was only at a business lunch after he had sealed a lucrative real estate deal. He wasn't mean but he liked to consider himself 'careful'.

As the drinks waiter arrived to open the bottle, the restaurant hostess escorted Estelle to the table and both men stood respectfully. Estelle, to their surprise, looked almost nice. She had applied a little make-up, which tended to soften her features, she wore a two-piece blue suit, the jacket of which was a rather attractive blue floral pattern and, of course, the compulsory, black low-heeled court shoes. Her hair was still pulled back severely but in the soft light of the restaurant, she looked reasonably passable.

They ate, drank, laughed and chattered about the events of the day, remembering some of the more humorous and frightening experiences, and were soon into the second bottle of Piper-Heidsieck, and becoming very relaxed in each other's company. Penny told how she had been accosted by a lecherous old devil with a wheeled walker, who chased her around the office until a sympathetic lady sitting in a chair waiting for her interview, stuck her sun-shade in the wheels and sent the old devil flying head first into the lap of another old codger, who immediately exploded to his feet thinking he was being attacked. The old codger pushed the old devil off him and immediately went into a pugilistic stance, jabbing his fists in the air, snorting and wiping his nose, as one would under the circumstances.

Obviously the old codger was an ex-boxer, but now, with his bottle-top glasses that somehow clung onto his pugilistic nose, he couldn't see very well and was doing a lot of air punching and bobbing and weaving in a circle. Beryl, the ex-security lady took charge. She whipped her .38 revolver out of her capacious handbag, grabbed the old codger around the throat, pushed the gun up his nose and said, 'Okay, cool it, gran'pa. Just take it nice and steady and no one'll get hurt.' At the same time, painful yells of 'Ow! Ow!' were coming from the old devil on the floor because the old codger was standing on his hand.

All was soon settled; the old devil was helped back up on his feet and given back his walker, and he retreated back to his seat, complaining about his arthritis, and the old codger settled down next to Beryl, who returned her weapon to her handbag, but kept a very wary eye on him.

Estelle told of the middle-aged gentleman who obviously had taken a fancy to her and tried to hit her. The others were shocked, which seemed to surprise her, until Penny corrected her saying, 'No, Estelle, he didn't try to hit you, he tried to hit ON you.'

'Oh,' said Estelle. 'Well, whatever, but it was very unpleasant.' She gave a little burp and giggled her apologies. Estelle was obviously not a seasoned drinker.

Aubrey said that maybe they should consider Beryl as one of the tenants as she'd be very handy for security in the block. Charles said that they should also consider Alec, the roo shooter, for the same reason. They decided to finalise the tenancy list and contact the successful applicants the next morning.

At the end of the evening, Aubrey gave a lovely speech, thanking them all for their hard work, saying he thought they would all make a wonderful team, and proposed a toast. 'To the success of the launching of the Twilight Escort Agency!' They all stood and raised their glasses.

'And all who sail on her!' added Charles.

'Hear, hear!' said Penny.

'Fuckin' oath!' said Estelle, slumping back onto her chair.

By the time they'd finished their after-dinner coffee, Charles and Penny were primed up and ready for the club crawl, but Aubrey and Estelle begged off, Aubrey saying he was tired after their big day and Estelle still giggling a lot and claiming she needed her beauty sleep. Charles couldn't agree more with her and, bidding them goodnight, he and Penny left for the clubs, 'or maybe the Casino,' Charles was heard saying, as they disappeared toward the exit.

Aubrey paid the bill, wincing at the total, and then said he would see Estelle home. She declined graciously saying she was 'perfectly culpable of seeing herself hooome'. But Aubrey insisted, taking her gently but firmly by the arm and escorting her out. She managed to avoid all but one pot-plant, which, she claimed had jumped out at her. 'I think that pot-plant was hitting ON me,' she declared, giggling.

Estelle was smiling but very quiet on the drive home. When they arrived outside her house, Charles was delighted at the modest but neat dwelling, with a charming front garden full of roses, shrubs and other flowering plants that bordered the curving, cobbled path and front porch. He was about to compliment her on the lovely home when Estelle suddenly threw her arms around his neck and planted a fairly moist kiss on his cheek saying, 'Oh, Mr Aubrey, I've had such a lubly ebening. Fank you sooooo much.' With that, she flung open the car door and weaved her way up the front path barely missing the red and green garden gnome and the green terracotta frog.

At that instant, and to his surprise, Aubrey became aware of a pleasant vibration flooding his loins. He smiled to himself somewhat sheepishly, turned the ignition key, started the motor and drove off. But the vibration continued until he suddenly realised he had switched his mobile phone in his pants pocket to 'vibrate' while they were in the restaurant. Being a good citizen, he pulled the car off the road onto the verge and scrabbled in his pocket for the phone. 'Hello, Aubrey Acres speaking.'

'Hello, Aubrey, my little darling, Mumsie here.'

Aubrey was shocked, receiving a call from his mother at such a late hour. 'Mumsie! How are you? Or more to the point, where are you?'

'I'm at the airport in Delhi, darling, and I have to catch an over-night train to Mount Abu, in Rajasthan, so I thought I'd give you a call to let you know so you wouldn't be worried.'

'Mumsie, what the hell are you doing in India?'

'Darling, I think I've found God. Well, I don't mean I'm actually travelling with him, I mean, not in person.'

Aubrey closed his eyes in weariness and sighed. 'Oh, Mumsie.'

'Now, don't be like that, darling. I met this marvellous man in Manchester: he's a member of a spiritual sect called the Brahma Kumaris and he invited me to a wonderful spiritual retreat in Madhuban. Well, it's not actually *in* Madhuban, it's on a mountain top just above Madhuban.'

Aubrey tried to interrupt but there was no stopping her. 'Mumsie ...'

'It's like an ashram and it sounds marvellous. The actual retreat is called Gyan Sarovar, which is a sort of retreat for Westerners, and he says it's frightfully spiritual and relaxing.'

'Mumsie ...'

'And he's taking me to the World Spiritual University in Madhuban, which is just down the mountain a bit. Just think, darling, Mumsie might be going back to University if everything works out all right.'

'But Mumsie ...'

'Mind you, I think to attend the University you have to be a vegetarian and celibate so that could be a bit of a draw-back.'

'But I thought you were a vegetarian anyway,' Aubrey managed to squeeze in.

'I am, darling. It's the other thing that could be the problem.'

'Mumsie ...'

'Now you mustn't worry, darling, I'll be just fine. I've bought some heavenly, spiritual, white silk Punjabi and kurta pyjamas to wear. They were a bit plain so I've added lots of silver sequins.'

'Mumsie, listen!' Aubrey almost shouted to get her attention. 'I've got some news that may interest you. My partner, Charles, you remember him, we were at Timbertop together – English? Well, he's moved out here and we've converted a block of apartments I own into an over-fifties establishment and we've attached an escort agency to it and ...'

'Oh, Aubrey, you've opened up a geriatric knock shop?' She sounded thrilled. 'How wonderful!'

'No, Mumsie, it's NOT a knock shop! It's a no-sex escort agency! It's for lonely older people who don't have anyone to take them out. It's just for company, not sex!'

'Oh,' said Pomegranate, sounding most disappointed. 'How nice – and how very *you*, darling.'

'And I was thinking, well hoping really, that maybe you'd like to come home and live in one of the apartments. It's not a retirement village,' he added quickly, 'it's right in the middle of all the action. You'd love it, I'm sure.'

There was a long pause, and then, 'The line seems to be breaking up, darling, I can't quite hear you. And there's so much noise in the airport here.'

'I said,' Aubrey almost shouted into the phone, 'It's not ...'

'It's no good, dear, can't hear a thing. Got to go now and catch the train. Lovely talking to you. I'll be in touch soon with all the news.'

The line started crackling almost as if Pomegranate was scrunching tissue paper at the other end.

'What's your new mobile number, I'll ring you? Your last one's been disconnected it seems … Mumsie?… Mumsie?'

But it was no use, the line had gone dead.

Chapter 10

They all sat around the conference table in the back room discussing the list of possible tenants. It was decided that Charles would move back into one of the rear ground floor apartments and act as a sort of on-site manager. They finally decided on the most suitable tenants and, as it turned out, all of them were also interested in joining the escort agency. There was no doubt Charles had a lot to do with the choice, but Aubrey wouldn't budge on a couple of his selections. Finally, everybody was in agreement.

Then they got onto possible nom de plumes for the escorts, of which there were surprisingly many.

'Now, let's see,' said Aubrey, referring to the list in front of him, 'we've got a Shaylene, a Charlene – obviously her mother had been an avid *Neighbours* fan – a Raelene, a Doreen, a Loreen and, would you believe a Valvoline.'

'Her father was obviously a mechanic,' said Charles.

'So,' said Aubrey, 'I think we should all write a list of nom de plumes that we could use for the individual escorts – something attractive.'

'And enticing,' said Charles. 'What about Bubbles and Chi Chi, Hottie Hatti, Madam Lash, Handcuff Hannah, and Floozie Foot Fetish?' he suggested.

'I think not,' said Estelle, disapprovingly.

'I think we need names unconnected to your previous establishments,' said Aubrey.

Charles shot him a hurt and disapproving look.

'But they should sound –' Penny searched for the word, '*intriguing*, don't you think? Like ... Wanda?'

'Wanda-Lust,' Charles beamed. 'I like it!'

'I think we should be looking at names like ... Raoul, or Pierre, or Alexander,' broke in Estelle, ignoring the flippancy.

'Not for the women, Estelle. Mind you, we could call Beryl the security guard Butch Beryl.'

'I meant for the *men*, Mr Charles,' replied Estelle patiently, 'and I don't think we'll be getting many bookings for Beryl anyway. She's been selected, as you say, mainly for security.'

'A lot of chaps out there like a bit of "rough trade", Estelle, believe me,' said Charles with the voice of experience.

It was decided that Charles would design and organise the website for the agency. From his research into the subject the others were amazed at the prices the top end of the market escorts were charging.

'Up to and over two or three thousand dollars an hour?' Aubrey said, astounded, almost choking on the words.

'There's no way we could think of charging anywhere near that much,' Estelle said, horrified. 'They'd lose their pension.'

'I'll read you a bit of blurb from the web about one of the escorts on offer,' said Charles, picking out a sheet of paper from his briefcase. 'Katriona – This luscious blonde, originally from Sydney, loves to have fun and frolic in the Queensland sun. Like the rare diamond she is, she also loves to experiment and experience life in its endless facets. She is open-minded, adventurous, and ensures that the service she offers guarantees absolute fulfilment. Her long, ash-blonde hair is excitingly soft to the touch, her silky smooth, tanned skin is sure to excite the senses of any red-blooded male, her passionate green eyes hold the secrets to the mysteries of the Karma Sutra and beyond. Her velvet soft mouth entices and excites.

'The stunning Katriona guarantees to lead you into a world of erotic passion and ecstasy.'

Laying the piece of paper on the table in front of him he continued, 'It then goes on and lists her age, height, weight, bust size, occupation …'

'Well, we know what that must be,' sneered Estelle.

'Hobbies and interests,' continued Charles. 'And, of course, her rates, which incidentally, in this case is three thousand dollars an hour.'

The others were stunned and Penny piped in with, 'I'm obviously in the wrong trade,' and went back to studying the photos of their escorts.

'The point is, said Charles, 'we will have to come up with something similar for the biographies on our website.

'You must be joking,' scoffed Aubrey.

'I mean not quite so erotic,' said Charles. 'We will need to "colour" the biogs, just a little, mind you. We don't want to get sued by the clients for misrepresentation. If we say Fatima is a Raquel Welsh look-alike, when she really looks more like Dame Flora Robson, we may be in trouble. And the photographs must be at least, recognisable – maybe just a little air-brushing,' he added.

'I think we might leave that side of it to you, Charles,' said Aubrey. 'But I must have the right of veto. It's not that I don't trust you, Charles,' he said, lying through his teeth, 'but two heads are better than one.'

'We've got a couple of those in here too,' said Penny indicating the pile of photographs.

'And what do you think we should charge?' asked Estelle.

'Seven-fifty,' said Penny.

'Seven hundred and fifty dollars an hour?' cried Aubrey, turning a little scarlet.

'No,' replied Penny. 'Seven dollars fifty cents an hour. And that's only for the really good ones,' she added. 'And seven dollars flat if they don't have their own teeth.'

The meeting drew to a close and just as Charles was leaving, he turned at the door and said to Aubrey, 'I think we have to aim for the top end of clients, Aubs – business men and women, millionaires preferably, rich, self-funded retirees with big super payouts, that sort.'

'That's not exactly what I had in mind,' Aubrey said, a little wistfully. 'I imagined more sad, lonely, ordinary people who wanted a little joy in their lives.'

74

'Well, we'll try for both and fix the rates accordingly, depending on the client,' said Charles as he retired to his office to get his creative juices running.

Chapter 11

As it happened, their first client arrived before Charles had actually completed the website. Her name was Mrs Barrington, a delightful, well-spoken lady who had heard about the agency through a friend who had been interested in renting one of the apartments. Aubrey was out on another real estate-related job, and Estelle was out picking up Aubrey's dry cleaning, and Charles was busy working on the website and told Penny that she should handle the inquiry for practice.

This was her first opportunity to show that she was indeed capable of dealing with clients, and she attacked the job with fervour, personality, efficiency and charm oozing from every pore. She sat Mrs Barrington down and asked exactly what the lady had in mind.

Mrs Barrington explained that she had been invited to a barbecue by a lady friend and told to bring a male companion along to make up the numbers. Mr Barrington had died two years ago, leaving his wife alone in what to her was a strange state, as they had only moved to the Gold Coast from Melbourne a few months prior to his fatal heart attack. Since then she hadn't made many friends and those she had were all women. She and her husband had always been a socially active couple and she missed the outings she'd always enjoyed. So now she had decided to do something about it and approach the agency to see what they had to offer.

It was to be a 'mystery' barbecue, smart casual dress, in the garden of a very palatial address in Broadbeach. Mrs Barrington wanted to surprise her hostess by arriving with a mysterious, tall, dark, handsome escort to show that she still had what it took to attract handsome men, and if her hostess was a little envious, all the better.

As the office and records were still in the process of being organised, Penny scrambled around, trying to match files with photographs of a selection of escorts to present to Mrs Barrington. She dragged a pile out onto her desk and began sorting through them and in the process, she managed to get a few files mixed up but was finally able to suggest to her client that perhaps 'Antonio,' would be perfect for her. He was indeed, well built, tall, dark and handsome and a thoroughly charming, well-mannered gentleman, who had led an adventurous life in the deserts and rainforests of outback Australia. The fact that the names on the biogs and photographs had been mismatched and Alexander-nee-Alec the roo shooter, was being confused with Antonio-nee-Tony, the Maori ex-abalone fisherman, with an accent that was almost unintelligible to an English-speaking person, went completely undetected. Mrs Barrington agreed that Antonio would be perfect for the occasion.

Terms were agreed upon with Penny going for the best deal she could manage, which Mrs Barrington readily agreed to. The files and photographs were pushed to one side, the date was set, the service confirmed and Mrs Barrington went on her way quite satisfied and very excited about her forthcoming daring assignation with the attractive Antonio.

Penny, very pleased with herself, had mistakenly picked up Tony's file and immediately emailed him, booking him for the job, and efficiently entered the details onto his record sheet.

The mistake wasn't discovered until the morning of the barbecue when Tony, or Antonio, arrived at the office for his final briefing and wardrobe check. He walked into the office looking like he'd just disembarked from his abalone boat after ten days at sea in a cyclone. He wore a pair of stained and dirty faded blue pants, a torn, faded brown T-shirt and a pair of equally dirty runners, with a lace in only one runner. His naturally unruly, black, curly hair exploded from his head as if from an extreme shock, but was thankfully covered by a stained hooded jacket in green and blue check.

'G'day, bro,' he said, 'I'm here for me date.'

Aubrey, Charles, Penny and Estelle were all in the reception area to witness this rather stunning entrance and for a moment all went into immediate shock.

Penny said, 'What are you doing here?'

'You emailed me,' replied Tony. 'I gotta date, girlie.'

The others all looked to Penny, who was standing with her mouth sagging open.

'No, not you, Tony, I booked Alexander.'

'No, girlie, you booked me. I got the email here.' He dug in his pocket and produced the email. 'I jist got beck from a feshin' trup.'

'Right,' said Charles. 'I think there's been a little mistake.'

'No way, bro, I em booked for a barbecue an' I'm all drissed and ready to go.'

'Estelle, ring Alec! Now. Quickly!' barked Charles.

Estelle raced to the phone and dialled frantically but there was no answer.

'Penny,' Charles said, grabbing her by the arm and dragging her into his office, 'could I have a word?'

In the office, he turned to her furiously. 'What the hell have you done?'

Penny was on the verge of tears as she wailed, 'I'm so sorry, Charlie – Mr Charles. I must've got confused. I thought I'd booked Alexander!'

'Well, you obviously didn't, did you? You've booked that Maori misfit, haven't you? He shouldn't even be on the books. He was marked as a reject. And just who is the client expecting?'

'Well, him, Tony, I expect.'

Charles groaned. 'This is our very first booking. What do you think Mrs Barrington is going to say when that turns up? She'll have a fit! She'll think he's there to deliver her halibut and prawns, not take her to a society function! We'll just have to ring and cancel. We can't let him loose on her. We'll be a laughing stock.'

'It's too late to cancel, Mr Charles, that will ruin our reputation too,' she continued to wail. 'Maybe we could clean him up a bit.'

'We'd have to use paint stripper and bleach on him to do any good,' screamed Charles. 'And he's black! Or haven't you noticed under that six inches of grime?'

'Oh, I'm so sorry, Charlie – Mr Charles. Well, she did say she wanted someone who was tall, dark and handsome.'

'Tall, dark and handsome is not the same as medium height, black and ugly, young lady.'

'He didn't look so bad in his photo,' said Penny. 'Maybe he's just having an ugly day. It happens to me sometimes.'

'If you ever wake up looking like that, don't even bother coming in,' said Charles.

Just then the door opened and Aubrey and Estelle entered.

'We've just been discussing the situation, Charles,' said Aubrey, 'and Estelle thinks all may not be lost.'

'Mr Charles,' said Estelle, 'we can't cancel at this late stage and we can't get anyone else now, so I suggest we improvise.'

'What are you talking about, Estelle, improvise from what, to what and with what?'

'Well, I've been looking at him a little closer while you've been in here and I think underneath the outward appearance, there may just be something worth salvaging.'

'And what would that be, Estelle, the hooded jacket or the revolting runners?'

'No, they've got to go, but I've been thinking. If you take him back to your apartment and give him a shave, a good shower and scrub-down and dress him in some of your designer clothes – after all, he is about the same size as you, except his waist is a bit smaller –' Charles gasped at the effrontery but chose to ignore the remark, '– and Penny can cut and style his hair, she's very good at that. We may just get away with it.'

'But the voice,' cried Charles, 'it's like a bad foreign movie and we can't send him out with sub-titles. And manners! He hasn't got any! He's got all the social graces of a baboon at the Royal enclosure at Ascot.'

'We haven't really got any other option,' said Estelle.

There was a tense pause with Estelle looking at Aubrey and Aubrey looking at Charles, who had sunk to his knees with his head in his hands, groaning.

'Charles, let's give it a try,' said Aubrey quietly.

Charles slowly raised his head and looked at them, defeated. 'Oh, all right, we'll try but I warn you, if he has to wear my clothes, I'll have to burn them later. If we're sued for wilful damage to Polite Society, I'll deny everything.'

'All right, troops, to the trenches!' cried Estelle, as if rallying the Diggers to go 'over the top' for their final charge.

'Where we goin', bro?' Tony asked as they forcibly dragged him out of the office and around to Charles' apartment.

'We're going to clean you up and dress you properly so you won't disgrace us,' said Charles rather roughly as Tony protested and struggled.

'What yer talkin' about, bro?' he said. 'I'm takin' a womin to a barbecue, for Chris' sake. I allus dress cesual for a barbecue, bro.'

'Not that casual,' said Charles. 'This is a respectable barbecue, with a very respectable lady, at a very respectable house, in a very respectable neighbourhood.'

'So I'll be respictable. Jes' you wait an' see.'

They dragged him into Charles' apartment, stripped him of his clothes and virtually threw him into the shower, telling him to shave and scrub himself, and not come out until he was as clean as the driven snow.

'Bit difficult, bro, wrong colour for that,' said Tony.

Charles went into his walk-in robe and sorted through his clothes and finally chose a pair of white Gaz Man slacks, a yellow silk, short-sleeved shirt, white socks and a pair of white, Italian leather, hand-made slip-on shoes. Tears came to his eyes as he laid them on the bed, ready for Tony to put on.

'What a waste,' he muttered through his tears. 'Designer labels before swine.'

After Tony had showered and shaved, Aubrey took over to oversee the actual dressing because Charles just couldn't bring himself to face the gruesome task. A few minutes later Aubrey called out for Penny and Estelle to come in and attend to Tony's hair. Charles collapsed onto his leather couch and tried to clear the awful scenario running through his mind.

After a short time the bedroom door opened. Aubrey, Estelle and Penny stood like a guard of honour with their hands raised towards the bedroom and in unison they shouted, 'Da dah!'

Through the open doorway emerged a vision of sartorial splendour: Tony had suddenly turned into 'Antonio the Magnificent'.

'What yer think, bro?' he said, beaming at Charles, who had suddenly gone into shock. 'Pritty good eh.'

The white slacks clung to a very well-rounded, firm bum, and his subtle but impressive 'Mound of Manhood'. The shirt, tastefully open at the throat to the second button, revealing a very expensive gold chain, hinted at a still-muscular chest and biceps. The face was as smooth as a baby's bottom and looked ten years younger, and the hair was shampooed, cut and trimmed to perfection.

Charles was absolutely astounded by the transformation.

'Brilliant!' he yelled as he jumped to his feet, 'Absolutely bloody brilliant! And that gold chain is perfect.'

'So it should be,' said Estelle, 'it's one of yours.'

Charles hid his horror extremely well under the circumstances. 'It all comes back, remember.' He sniffed the air. 'And the Calvin Klein aftershave.'

Estelle nodded. 'Sorry, I think we went a bit too far with that.'

'And I suppose those are my socks you've got rolled up and stuck down the front of your pants.'

'No,' said Tony with offended pride, 'Thet's all mine, bro.'

Quickly changing the subject Charles pronounced, 'I think the shirt should be tucked in.'

Aubrey sidled up to Charles and whispered in his ear, 'We had to leave it hanging out to cover the pucker in the waist of the pants. The waist was a little ...'

Charles jumped in to cover the end of Aubrey's tactless remark. 'Well, not bad, not bad, I suppose. It is the fashion nowadays. We may just get away with it, if you don't open your mouth.'

'What you mean, bro?'

'Well, for a start, there will be no more "bro's" in your conversation, neither will there be any "Eh" or "ay's" at the end of every sentence and under no circumstance will you mention any number between five and seven. Is that clear?'

Tony looked mystified.

'Well, off you go,' said Charles. 'And remember, the fate of the agency is in your hands. You do have suitable transport, I suppose?' he added.

''Course, bro ...sorry, bro, I mean Mistah ... sir. Don' you worry, I hev bin out with proper people before, y'know.'

He turned to Penny, 'You sure I don' look like a poof in this gear?'

Charles spluttered in high dudgeon.

84

'You look marvellous, Antonio,' she smiled. 'If you were ten years younger I'd go for you myself.'

'Whin I was tin years younger, you would've bin in the queue, girlie.'

And with that, he turned and walked out, carrying the hopes of the agency on his broad shoulders.

Chapter 12

It had been two days since Antonio's rendezvous and as they had not heard a word from either party they feared the worst. Antonio was not answering his phone or returning emails and Mrs Barrington's phone was constantly busy.

'Probably talking with her lawyer,' proclaimed Charles, despondently.

Aubrey said something to the effect that you can always expect teething problems in a new business, and suggested that Charles get on with designing the website. Charles told him that he'd had the photographs done and it was going to cost more for the airbrushing than it was for the photographer.

Later that morning, Charles was in his office working on the biogs for the website and was obviously having trouble. He buzzed the intercom and asked Penny to come in.

'For my sins, I'm working on a suitable biog piece for Beryl, the security misfit,' he said as soon as she entered. 'She says on her application form she would like to be called "Bianca", can you imagine? And in her statistics column, she says she is five foot three inches tall, wears a size twenty-two dress or slacks and has a twenty-four G-cup bra size? Is that possible or is it a misprint?'

'No, it's probably right,' Penny said, unfazed.

'Twenty-four G? Do they make that size?'

'She probably has them tailor-made at Windsurf Sail Manufacturers,' said Penny.

'My God, she could be Lady Celia's little sister,' Charles exclaimed. 'And in her "Interests and Hobbies" column she has listed football, weight lifting, game fishing, shooting and wrestling. Do you think we'll have a call for that?'

'Well, you never know,' said Penny. 'That is a misprint about the wrestling. I think it's supposed to be mud wrestling. In the biog you could say "Interested in Ecological Soil Conservation". It's nice to have a varied choice of escorts though, don't you think?'

Just then, Estelle buzzed through and said, 'Mr Charles, I think you and Penny might like to come out here for a minute. Mr Aubrey's on his way. Mrs Barrington is out here wanting to talk about her experience with Antonio at the barbecue.'

Penny and Charles looked at each other in fear and trepidation, sighed and slowly made their way out to the reception area, girding themselves for the tirade that was sure to follow.

Mrs Barrington was sitting in a chair at Estelle's desk. She smiled politely as they approached. Aubrey was hovering behind her.

'Mrs Barrington, I'm Charles Wellington, Mr Acre's partner, and I must apolo—'

'How lovely to meet you both,' cut in Mrs Barrington. 'I was going to phone, but I felt a personal visit was more in keeping with what I had to say.'

'Well, I do hope your experience wasn't too disappointing for you, and if it was, may I say–'

'Disappointing?' Mrs. Barrington cried. 'It was absolutely fabulous!'

Charles, Aubrey, Estelle and Penny stared at her, and each other, in amazement.

'How terribly brilliant of you all to go to so much trouble,' she said. 'How on earth did you do it? How did you manage to get the inside information? I mean, to find out that the mystery barbecue was actually going to be a hangi? And to supply me with the most charming Kiwi escort was a stroke of genius!'

The others could only stare at her.

'I must say, when he arrived and escorted me to his campervan, I will admit I was a little puzzled and I might add, just a little concerned at the time, but I thought, What the hell, you wanted to live life on the edge, Bella, so go with the flow.'

'It went well?' Charles stammered.

'Well?' she exclaimed in disbelief. 'It was superb! All the catering staff were dressed in their national Maori costumes, and they even did a welcoming haka, and traditional dances to entertain us. And Antonio joined in! He was beautifully dressed for the occasion; in fact, so well dressed and neat, at first I wondered if he might be a homosexual. But as I soon found out,' she giggled girlishly, 'he was anything but. And I know I asked for

88

someone tall, dark and handsome, but I didn't think he looked quite that dark in his photograph. In fact I didn't think it was the same man you showed me at all,' she said turning to Penny and laughing.

Penny returned the laugh but with a slight edge of hysteria.

'But of course, I only saw the picture once and only briefly, and I know my eyesight is getting a little unreliable. But I was sure you told me he'd travelled a lot in the desert. I think your file may need updating, dear, he actually owns a fleet of fishing boats in New Zealand.'

Charles and Aubrey were still agog in amazement but Estelle and Penny had started to relax and were enjoying the moment enormously.

'I'll attend to that immediately, Mrs Barrington,' said Penny contritely.

'It turned out that he knew everybody in the catering company by their first names, in fact he claimed some of them as relatives. And when he saw the hangi pit he told the head chef that the hangi rocks were not good enough and said he had a much more superior set in the campervan, and he grabbed a couple of the lads and went off to fetch them! Apparently he carries them everywhere he goes, just in case. And he has this special blanket that he wets down to throw over the hangi for extra steam or something. It had a strange sort of fishy smell but the food was delicious.'

'And his manners?' asked Charles, tentatively.

'Perfect,' said Mrs Barrington, 'a perfect gentleman. And he was so amusing! His accent was delightful. He kept slipping back into his Maori accent whenever he was telling us a funny story. He was certainly a hit with all the ladies, I can tell you. They were so jealous of me. It was wonderful.'

She hesitated, as if she wanted to say something but wasn't quite sure.

'I'm sorry, I have to admit, I eventually had to confess to Cheryl, she's my friend who was the hostess. I swore her to secrecy but I know what a blabbermouth she is. I told her about coming here, about how I met Antonio. It'll probably be all over the coast by tomorrow. I'm so sorry.'

'Not at all!' piped in Aubrey, delightedly. 'I hope it will bring in more business for us.'

'Oh, it's sure to,' said Mrs Barrington. She paused for breath and then remembered what she meant to ask them. 'Oh, and I've been invited to an Alaskan party next week, I don't suppose you have an Eskimo on your books?'

'Sadly, no,' said Estelle, 'But we'll see what we can dig up.'

Mrs Barrington stood ready to leave. 'Oh, no, I want him alive,' she laughed, delighted at her little joke. 'Well, certainly as alive as Antonio.' She giggled again at the memories of her naughty encounter. 'Perhaps he might be available again. He'd pass for an Eskimo, don't you think?' She moved to the door and turned, 'Do keep in touch, and once again, thank you so much. I'll look forward to seeing you all again quite soon. No doubt I'll receive my account in due course.'

'It's in the mail,' said Estelle, as she ushered her to the door. 'And thank you so much for bothering to come in personally.'

She returned to the other three and she said, 'I don't suppose you have a fur anorak in your wardrobe, do you, Mr Charles?' They all laughed in blessed relief and threw their arms around each other in excitement and danced around in a little circle.

'I always knew Antonio had it in him, from the moment we met,' said Charles. 'And he can keep the clothes. – But not the gold chain,' he said as an afterthought.

Later that afternoon, Antonio arrived at the office and Penny and Estelle greeted him warmly, patted him on the back, and told him how marvellous he was, and how Mrs Barrington had been delighted with his company. He was very cool about the attention and compliments but secretly very pleased with himself. Estelle suddenly noticed that he was still wearing the same outfit that he'd worn to the barbecue and it was filthy. Immediately jumping to the conclusion that he'd spent the last two days with Mrs Barrington, rolling around on a mud flat somewhere, she frowned at him and said in an admonishing tone, 'Tony, you haven't changed Mr Charles' clothes, and they're in a dreadful state. You and Mrs. Barrington didn't …?'

'What you talkin' about, womin, eh? I drove the lovely lady home to her place efter the hangi, and then went straight out to the Spet to do some fushin' with me cuz an' a few mates. They wuz cookin' at the hangi, an' we found out what the tide was doin,' an' knew it wuz a full moon an' a perfect tide for the tailor runnin,' so we've bin there ivver since. Had a few drunks an' got a shut load of fush, too. Thought I'd better chuck it un an' come an' tell yus the hangi was a bug success.'

'So we heard, Antonio, congratulations,' said Estelle. 'But I don't think Mr Charles would be too happy about the clothes, so why don't you go home and change, and drop the clothes into the drycleaners and we'll pick them up later.'

'Fair enough, missus – oh, an' would you guv this beck to 'im please.' He reached into his pocket and dragged out the gold neck chain and handed it to her. 'Me mates gave me a shut load o' shut about wearin' thet, eh.'

He turned and sauntered out of the office, a Maori chieftain in anyone's eyes.

Chapter 13

Estelle read, *'If you are looking for a strong, flexible, athletic type, then Bianca's the woman for you. Bianca loves sports and can often be found on the sideline of big sporting events. Her fitness is imperative to her, as it was during her career as a policewoman, and later as a member of a professional security company. She can often be found working out at the local gym. Her full figure elicits amazement; with strong, firm muscles, and exotic features that cast a sense of disbelief in the beholder. Yet with all her physical attributes, she has a friendly, down-to-earth sense of humour and a natural, motherly, protective instinct. Heads are sure to turn when she accompanies you on your outing.'*

'Well, what do you think?' said Charles, as he retrieved the biog piece from Estelle.

'I suppose you've got most of the facts sort of right,' she said dubiously, 'but you're wrong about finding her on the sidelines of sporting events; she actually plays in her local rugby team – forward position, I believe.'

'Oh dear,' said Charles. 'Well, I think, in Beryl's case, I can use a little poetic license.'

'Have you finished all the others?' asked Estelle.

'Just about. I was leaving Beryl's till last. It was quite a challenge.'

'The photographs came out really well,' said Estelle. 'I hardly recognised some of them.'

'Well, I couldn't put them in as they really look, now could I? They're just a teaser. It'll be up to you and Penny to actually sell them.'

'We've actually received a lot of inquiries,' said Estelle. 'We've already booked Alec, I mean, Alexander, for three dinner dates, and Fred, that's Raoul, as an escort for the Queensland Ballet's performance of *Giselle*.'

'Did you get the right names and photographs this time?' he asked provokingly with a smile.

'I must remind you, Mr Charles, it was Penny, your – ahem – niece, who made that unfortunate mistake,' she said a little testily, 'but she really can't be blamed because the files and photographs were in a bit of a mess at that early stage. But I can assure you, everything is in order now and there will be no further confusion.'

'Thank you, Estelle, I'm sure you've got everything organised perfectly. Ah, this Alexander, who was he again?' He shuffled through the biogs on his desk.

'Alexander was Alec, remember? He's the roo shooter and crocodile hunter from the Territory.'

'Ah, yes, here he is,' he said, at last finding the biog he'd written, and started to read. *'Alexander is fondly known as Alexander the Great, and for a very good reason. He is six feet four inches tall,* – I think it's best to keep everything in imperial for the age group we're appealing to, don't you?' he said as he glanced up at Estelle.

'Whatever you think, Mr Charles.'

'He weighs in at thirteen stone, has intelligent but humorous deep brown eyes …'

'That sounds like he might have a funny squint, or one eye bigger than the other, Mr Charles.'

'Perhaps you're right,' Charles agreed. 'Maybe "fun loving"?'

Estelle nodded sagely.

'Right.' He picked up a pencil and made the correction, and continued, *'The many years he spent in the Outback hardened his muscles and his character, and bleached what is left of his hair. His adventurous spirit and outgoing personality make him a favourite for bush walking, mountain climbing, kayaking, desert trekking and water skiing. All he needs is a little help with his electric wheelchair. He is also …'*

'Just a minute, Mr Charles,' Estelle cut in. 'He doesn't use a wheelchair.'

'Doesn't he?' queried Charles.

She shook her head. 'I think you've got him mixed up with Max, the one we rejected.'

'Oh, right. I did think the mountain climbing and water skiing might have presented a bit of a challenge.'

'Not to mention the kayaking, bush walking and desert trekking,' she said a little wryly. 'No, he's perfectly fit and healthy, and also makes an excellent dinner companion or dancing partner.'

'Right,' he said again, ruling out the offending line and inserting Estelle's suggestions.

'Well, I'll leave you to it, Mr Charles, and you will remember to let me have a look at the other biogs you've written before you pass them on to Mr Aubrey, won't you? – Just so we have the facts right.'

'Of course,' said Charles. 'I wouldn't dream of leaving you out of the loop.'

She nodded and returned to her desk in Reception.

'In fact, I'd like to put the loop right around your scrawny neck,' Charles muttered as he went back to his alterations.

'Silly old fool,' Estelle muttered as she sat at her desk.

'Who?' asked Penny.

'Mr Charles, that's who. We'll have to check all of those biographies he's been writing otherwise we'll have Cyril being called Celestine, with long, shapely legs that look wonderful in fishnets and six-inch heels.'

Penny giggled. 'Well, he probably would. As long as Cyril had a wax job, and we could get a pair of high-heel shoes in a size fourteen.'

Just then, the front door opened and in walked a thin little old man with a walking stick. He was very well dressed in a neat, smart suit with an open-necked shirt and a smart Fedora hat. He came to the desk and Penny smiled and asked if she could help.

'I'd like to hire an escort,' he said gruffly.

'Of course, sir,' she said smiling, 'and for what kind of occasion?'

'Someone who's interested in sport, and she has to have strong legs.'

'What kind of sport do you have in mind,' asked Penny, a little puzzled.

'Football – NRL.'

'National Rugby League? And why does she need strong legs?' Penny asked.

'Well, she'd have to climb up into the bleachers, wouldn't she,' he replied.

Penny looked to Estelle for assistance. Estelle immediately said, 'Bianca! Bianca would be perfect for you.'

'Right, she'll do,' said the old man.

'But wouldn't you like to see a photo, I mean, so you'll know what she looks like?'

'Nah, doesn't matter,' said the old man, 'as long as she's strong.'

Penny got out a booking form and took down the details including the time and address Bianca was to collect him from. They discussed the fee, and rules and regulations that would apply. The 'no sex' regulation didn't seem necessary to stipulate, under the circumstances, seeing as Bianca wouldn't have much trouble handling a thin little old weakling with a walking stick.

The little old man, whose name turned out to be Reg, paid the deposit in cash from a bill roll from his pocket and left.

Penny and Estelle stared at each other in disbelief. Penny said, 'A booking for Bianca? I don't believe it.'

'It's a strange world we've found ourselves in, Penny,' said Estelle. 'But who are we to complain? Beryl gets a booking and we get our commission. We offered to show him a photo and biog, but he wasn't interested, so, if he gets a surprise when she turns up it's his own fault.'

'Surprise?' said Penny. 'He'll probably drop dead in shock.'

'Well, we have his deposit; and it's non-refundable, so what have we got to lose?'

Penny immediately got on the phone to Beryl and made the booking. Beryl, or 'Bianca,' wasn't a bit surprised and took down the details very professionally. She was a bit surprised at the time for the booking, which was very early in the morning, but suspected it was to go and see the local team, the Titans, training. Penny agreed that must be the case, and rang off.

On the day of the booking, Bianca arrived at the appointed address on time, in her aqua tracksuit, looking like one of the costumed mascots of the local team, and rang the front doorbell. After a few moments, the little old man opened the door and said, 'Who are you?'

'I'm Bianca, from the escort agency,' she said with a bright smile. 'You must be Reg.'

The little old man looked her up and down and said, 'Gawd, I bet you don't get much work. I thought you'd come to read the meter.'

'Now, don't be cheeky, you silly old bugger,' she said, as she pushed her way past him and into the living room. 'So, what sort of fun have we got in store this morning, eh, grandpa?'

The little old man explained to her that all he wanted was for her to queue up for tickets for the upcoming clash between the Titans and the Brisbane Broncos football teams. He was too frail to stand for all that time, he said, and would wait for her in the pub across the road until she got the tickets and delivered them back to him.

'And that's it?' she asked, amazed.

'That's it,' he replied.

'Well, listen to me, you silly old bugger, if I'm gunna have to stand for bloody hours so you can get your bloody tickets, you can bloody well pay for one for me too, and book me as your escort for the night game as well. Deal?'

He looked at her shrewdly for a few moments, summing her up, and then realised he'd got himself one strong and determined Amazon warrior to deal with. So finally he said, 'Deal, you tough old broad.'

'And we only go in the best seats, right?' she said, laying it on the line. 'And a nice supper after the game,' she added as a clever afterthought

'Supper?' he roared.

'Supper, you stingy old bastard,' she said. 'Don't think you've got yourself a cheap broad here. And, I don't do Specials or Extras.'

They stared at each other like two prize-fighters, sizing each other up in the ring.

He was the first to back down, 'All right, you thieving old cow, supper after the game.'

Bianca's face broke into a wide grin of triumph. 'Thanks, you skinny little runt, it'll be a pleasure.'

Bianca rang Estelle after she'd dropped Reg back home and told her the story of how successful the 'date' had been, naturally without including the finer details, and said she and the little old man had got on so well, he'd booked her again to go to the game with him, and had offered to take her to supper afterwards. Estelle was both surprised and delighted; surprised that Reg hadn't fainted when he saw her, and delighted that Bianca had got herself another booking.

Maybe Bianca had hidden charms they hadn't recognised previously.

She rushed into Aubrey's office to tell him of Bianca's success and he was as surprised as she, agreeing that obviously Bianca had hidden qualities that neither of them had detected. Aubrey said they should discover just what this secret attraction was as they may be able to use it for future engagements. They decided that maybe they should do a little spying to watch her in action and discover this secret, so Aubrey suggested that perhaps he and Estelle should arrange to be present at the supper Bianca and Reg were going to after the game.

On the night of the game it was cold, wet and windy as Estelle and Aubrey entered the dining area of the pub, and it was obvious that there were quite a few other football fans who were also enjoying a drink and a bite to eat after the game. Aubrey cautiously peered around the doorway and almost immediately spotted the 'romantic couple' sitting and chatting at a table against the far wall.

As luck would have it, there was a table just becoming vacant nearby, behind a filigreed wooden screen, where they could sit unobserved by Bianca and Reg, and still be able to hear their conversation. Like two secret agents, they bobbed and darted through the rowdy crowd, temporarily hiding from time to time behind other patrons and pillars, until they arrived, unnoticed by Bianca and Reg, at the vacant table and sat.

The unlikely escort and her date were both drinking beer from a large, and by now half-empty, jug on the table, and Bianca was just finishing her Lamb Shanks on Mash, while Reg sucked his way through a Beef Burgundy Casserole. By sitting and awkwardly leaning their heads against the wooden screen, Aubrey and Estelle still had to strain to hear the conversation at the next table. To an observer, they looked like an elderly married couple suffering from a bad case of Congenital Torticollis, or twisted neck syndrome.

'So you were a cop?' Reg was saying to Bianca between slurps. 'That doesn't surprise me. But you're not now, are you?' He looked at her a little doubtfully.

'No, that was when I was younger. After that, I was a truck driver – Nomadic Interstate Truck Drivers, we were called. Mostly we did the Perth to Sydney run.'

'Get away!' said Reg, obviously impressed.

'Yeah, across the Nullarbor – dusty bitch of a track, that was. Me and a mate used to share the driving. On the road train convoys we had to leave a twenty-minute interval between the trucks to give the dust a chance to settle, otherwise you couldn't see.'

'I bet you've got a lot of funny stories though. And I bet there was a bit of hanky panky that went on in those cramped cabins, eh?' Reg winked lecherously.

'Only once,' said Bianca, 'and that was when some dyke sheila went for a bit of a grope. But I soon put her in her place, and that was in the toolbox next to the spare tyre.'

Reg nearly cacked himself.

Bianca drained her glass. 'Yeah, we had some funny times, and some not so funny.'

Reg signalled a waiter for another jug as Bianca continued.

'There was one young bloke in outback Queensland, real smart-ass he was, new to the job, knew everything, he was doing his first solo road-train with a load of cattle. You see, when you're driving in from the West, you can only go as far as Toowoomba, and they trans-ship into Brisbane from there in smaller trucks.'

Reg nodded, waiting expectantly.

'Well, this young kid thought he'd show the managers and the other drivers a thing or two, and decided he'd go straight through to Brissie. I think he'd been popping something. So, sure enough, he does get right into the middle of the city without the cops picking him up, and the next thing, they get a frantic call on the CB back at the office and the cops are going ballistic. Turns out the kid got stuck in the middle of town and couldn't turn around to get back out, and couldn't even turn into another street because the road train was so long! Traffic was banked up for miles!'

Reg was chuckling and shaking his head,

'So,' continued Bianca, 'they finished up having to hire a crane to get him out! You can imagine the stink that caused.'

Reg laughed and swallowed another half glass of beer. 'Why did you give it away?' he asked.

Bianca drained another half of her schooner and suddenly became thoughtful and a little morose. 'I got fed up with the long hours and ...' there was a long, thoughtful pause, '... a lot of shit went on in those days, probably still does.' There was another long pause before she suddenly said, 'I'd rather not talk about it.'

'Oh, go on,' Reg pleaded. 'You can tell me. We're old mates now; footy mates.'

She looked at him for a moment, took another swig of her beer and said, 'Okay, but this is very serious so I wouldn't want it to get out.'

'Cross me heart,' said Reg, putting down his beer to make the appropriate gesture.

Aubrey and Estelle leaned in even closer, trying to hear Bianca as she lowered her voice conspiratorially.

'Well, me and me mate were driving across the Nullarbor one night – well, he was driving – pitch black as usual but millions of stars in the sky, and suddenly we felt a bit of a bump and Verg said, "Jesus, I think I just hit somethin' lying on the road. It looked like an old man!" We slammed on the brakes and we got out of the cabin and ran back along the road to have a look.' She turned her head left and right to make sure she wasn't being overheard, and continued. Aubrey and Estelle were sipping their wine, as they listened enthralled.

'Sure enough, he was right, we'd hit this poor old Aboriginal man who must've been having a sleep on the road. They do that sometimes because it's nice and flat and warm.'

'He was probably pissed,' Reg volunteered.

'Well, he didn't smell too good, I can tell you, but there again, you wouldn't if you'd been hit by a truck, would you? Anyway, he was as dead as a wombat in a whirlpool. We were miles from anywhere and we didn't know what to do. So we decided we'd better bury the poor old bugger, so we dragged him over to the side of the road, got a shovel out of the tool-kit and dug him a bit of a grave and piled stones on top of him, so as the dingos wouldn't get an easy meal, and marked the spot on our map, so we could tell the cops in the first town we came to.'

For some reason, the picture she painted appealed to Reg's racist sense of humour and he started to chuckle.

'You ran over a boong having a kip in the middle of a highway?' he chortled incredulously.

'An Aboriginal person,' Bianca corrected him tersely. 'Don't get racist with me.'

Aubrey and Estelle sat horrified but enthralled as the story unfolded. Estelle took another couple of gulps of her wine.

'Well, anyway, it was morning by the time we got to the next town and we went straight to the police station to report what had happened. And, you won't believe this, but when we told the sergeant on duty, he was as cool as a cucumber. He said, "Oh, fuck, not another one. Where did this happen?"

'We showed him the spot on our map and he said, "Oh, Christ, that's fuckin' miles away. I'm not driving all that way for a dead Abo. And do you know how much paperwork is involved in this sort of thing? Listen, next time this happens, and it probably will, what you got to do is move your spare tyre, dump him in your toolbox – don't for God's sake put him in the cabin with you, he'll stink you out – and bring him back here, and I'll plant him in the backyard." '

This was now getting too much for Reg and he was trying desperately to stop himself from laughing and possibly pissing his pants. Aubrey was transfixed and Estelle was settling her nerves with more wine.

Bianca was now lost in the horror of past memories and tears began to form in her eyes. 'I said to the cop, "But what about his family or the rest of his tribe? Won't we have to tell them?"

' "No," said the cop, "for fuck's sake don't even think of it. They'll blame you for killing him and probably stick a fuckin' spear through you, or knock your noggin with a nulla nulla. Don't worry, they'll think he's just gone walkabout and won't miss him for years. No, just drive back out there, dig him up, stick him in the toolbox, and bring him back here, and I'll bury him out the back garden with the others."

' "The others?" I said to him. "You mean there's been others?"

'The cop just smiled and beckoned us out the back and pointed to his garden, with lots of green vegetables and healthy looking fruit trees. And he said, "Look at that, ever seen such a bonzer crop? They make great fertiliser." '

The tears started to roll down Bianca's cheeks as she recalled the vivid memory.

But this was the last straw for Reg who went into paroxysms of laughter, which caused him to cough and choke on his beer.

And this was also too much for Bianca, who never expected anyone could be so heartless and cruel.

She stood up and helped Reg to his feet, slapped him on the back to ease his coughing and, at the same time, with her other hand, which she'd balled into a fist, gave him a short, sharp jab to his jaw. Reg's eyes rolled back in their sockets and his knees started to buckle but Bianca grabbed him just before he hit the floor, lifted him up bodily and slung him over her shoulder.

The manageress came running up, agitated, because the action, as one could imagine, had caused a bit of a stir in the dining room, and said, 'Is your father all right, dear? Do you want me to get an ambulance?'

'No, he'll be all right,' said Bianca, brushing the tears from her cheek with her spare hand. 'He just got pissed and had a funny turn. It happens all the time. I'll just take the old bastard home and chuck 'im in his cot.'

And with that, she strode out the door, with an unconscious Reg dangling down her back, leaving a very concerned manager staring in their wake.

Aubrey and Estelle watched in disbelief.

'Well,' said Aubrey, after a moment. 'You've got to admit, she has a certain way about her.'

Estelle swamped down the last of her wine.

Again, Aubrey had to drive the tipsy Estelle home and help her to her front door. She gave him a long hug of thanks but was unable to speak, and disappeared through the doorway closing the door behind her.

Aubrey, still feeling a little unsettled and sorry for putting Estelle through such an upsetting time, turned and went back to his car. Again he got that strange vibration in his groin but realised, as before, it must be his mobile phone vibrating in his pocket. It's probably Mumsie calling again from some mountain top in India, he thought as he went to get the phone from his pocket. But he suddenly noticed the mobile phone wasn't in his pocket; it was lying on the dashboard of the car. But the vibration in his groin continued.

Chapter 14

The next morning Estelle was in a terrible quandary. She knew she had to ring Reg about the previous night's events, but didn't want him to know that she and Aubrey had been spying on them. She also desperately wanted to know how he was feeling this morning after his 'date' had knocked him unconscious. There was also the fear that he may even sue the agency. Finally she couldn't delay the moment any longer and determined that, seeing as Reg would obviously be furious, she would offer to cancel his debt for the agency fee as a conciliatory gesture.

She called his number and after a few moments Reg answered. 'Yeah, Reg here.'

'Oh, good morning, Reg, this is Ms Twigden from the Twilight Escort Agency, and I am just calling to see how you are this morning, and if you have any complaints with our service.'

'Complaints!' he roared, as Estelle winced in anticipation of the onslaught that was surely to follow. 'It was bloody marvellous!' he continued to roar. 'The Titans beat the Broncos by twenty-four to eighteen! It was great!'

Estelle's eyes sprang open in surprise. 'That's wonderful, Reg, but what about your escort?'

'Bloody ripper!' he raved. 'She's a great girl. She was cheering and swearing louder than the rest of the stadium. She was bonzer company.'

'And what about the supper afterwards?'

'Well, to tell you the truth, we had a couple of beers with our dinner and I think I must've given the elbow a bit of a nudge because I can't remember a thing after we'd eaten. I hope I didn't embarrass the little lady. She must've got me home all right though, because I woke up in me bed this morning, right as rain. What a bloody pearler she was. I must say though, I did have a bit of a headache when I woke up, and me jaw was a bit sore so I must've bumped into something. But your thoughtful little darling had even put a couple of Aspirin and a glass of water on my bedside table, ready for when I woke up. I tell you, Ms Twigden, you've got yourself a real treasure there, so you look after her. And I'll definitely be booking the Bonzer Bianca again.'

'Thank you, Reg, we do like to guarantee satisfaction from our escorts. We'll certainly look forward to hearing from you again.'

She hung up the phone with a sigh of relief that Pomegranate must have heard on the mountaintop in India.

'What happened?' asked Penny in eager amazement.

Estelle repeated the telephone conversation she'd just had with Reg and they both broke into uproarious laughter.

'Just goes to show you, there's always somebody out there for everybody,' said Penny.

At that moment Aubrey entered from the street and made his way to his office, with a rather tight, nervous nod and a smile to Penny, and an even more embarrassed smile to Estelle, who returned the smile but accompanied it with a blush, which at least brought some colour into her face. Aubrey also blushed and muttered, 'Would you come into my office, Estelle, when you've got a moment, we've got to discuss what happened last night.' With that he almost fled into his office and closed the interconnecting door.

Penny witnessed this strange exchange and said to Estelle, 'Allo, allo, and what did happen last night, ET?'

Estelle blushed even deeper and replied, 'I've already told you, Penny,' she said, quickly returning to the paperwork on her desk and changing the subject. 'Would you ring Bianca in apartment eight and ask her to drop in for a chat later on today?'

Penny smiled knowingly and nodded.

Later, when Estelle had recovered at least some of her composure, she went into Aubrey's office to tell him the surprising outcome of Bianca and Reg's date. Aubrey was thrilled that it had turned out so well. One could sense a little tension in the air so Aubrey tried to relieve it by asking Estelle if there were any further bookings in the offing. She rose to the occasion and told him that the business was certainly looking up now that their website was finally up and running, and word of mouth was starting to get about. In fact Alec, the roo shooter, had been booked for a bushwalking outing by a lovely lady named Gladys. Apparently Gladys was in her late fifties, another widow, whose husband, Ted, had died a few years ago after a heart by-pass operation had gone tragically wrong. The surgeon had joined the wrong arteries together so Ted's blood didn't know whether it was coming or going. Anyway, Gladys had received a huge payout from the surgeon's insurance company and was now living the high life.

Gladys was fit and healthy and was very much into exercise so opted for the bushwalking and rock-climbing excursion with Alexander the Great, nee Alec.

'I'm not a bit worried recommending Alexander to any of our lady clients,' Estelle said. 'He's terribly popular. His dinner dates have been wonderfully successful, with many follow-up bookings, and with his adventurous background, he's considered quite a catch. And he's also a great tenant in the apartments and gets on well with everyone.'

'Well, you certainly sound taken with him.' Aubrey sounded a little miffed.

'Oh, only in a strictly business sense, Mr Aubrey, I can assure you.'

Aubrey brightened up again. 'Well, that's great news. Wish we had a few more like him.' He paused for a moment then continued, 'You know, Estelle, I had serious doubts about going into this business, but it appears they were quite unfounded. God bless Charles, eh?'

'I hope He does, Mr Aubrey,' replied Estelle. 'If anybody needs blessing, Mr Charles certainly could do with it.'

'How's your mum?' said Aubrey, trying to change the subject and avoid an awkward moment.

'Oh, about the same. Still aiming a little high. And how's yours?'

'Also aiming high,' said Aubrey, 'on a mountain top in India, meditating. I hope the arthritis in her knees stands up to it. The thought of Mumsie sitting in the lotus position for too long fills me with horror. She's liable to get stuck sitting cross-legged on the top of the mountain and they'll have to hire a crane to get her down.'

Estelle smiled sympathetically and turned to leave. At the door she turned again, looking a little contrite, and said, 'Mr Aubrey, I do so apologise for my dreadful behaviour again last night. I don't know what comes over me. I must never drink wine when I'm out again. I just don't think I can handle it anymore.'

'Not at all!' Aubrey assured her. 'You were wonderful company. You certainly have nothing to be ashamed of. Let's not talk about it again.'

Estelle smiled, so very relieved. 'Oh, thank you, Mr Aubrey. Well, I'd better get back to work.'

She exited the office leaving Aubrey with what could only be described as a rather wistful smile on his face.

Chapter 15

When Estelle had taken the booking for the bushwalking excursion from Gladys, things had gone very smoothly. Gladys was a charming lady with a firm, generous figure and long fair hair done in a style that really suited her. However, Estelle did notice that Gladys wore a hearing aid and the hairstyle was designed to cover it, so she concluded Gladys was a little vain or perhaps sensitive about displaying it.

Of course, Alexander was the immediate choice to partner Gladys, and it was quickly confirmed when Gladys saw his photograph and read his biography. 'My,' she said, 'what a good-looking man; and so well built by the look of it.'

'Yes, he is one of our most popular escorts. You'll find he has excellent manners and a great deal of charm,' said Estelle.

'He sounds perfect,' said Gladys. 'Is he terribly expensive? I've been doing a little research on the web and some of the prices are exorbitant. Then I found your charming website and saw that your prices are far more reasonable.'

'Well, we are in a slightly different category to the other similar websites,' explained Estelle. 'Our services are not quite so … extensive.'

'Well, it certainly seemed to have everything to offer that I needed,' said Gladys.

So the booking was finalised and a deposit paid in cash and left obviously very excited about the forthcoming excursion with such a handsome escort.

The day after the event, Alexander was on the doorstep before the office even opened. He strode into the office in a stony mood, and stood facing Estelle, who was quite surprised at his obvious agitation.

'Don't ever make a booking for me with that woman again,' he flatly stated. 'She's a sex-crazed weirdo!'

'What are you talking about?' said Estelle. 'She seemed like such a lovely lady.'

'She might well be,' said Alexander, 'when she wears her bloody hearing aid!'

Estelle looked at him askance.

'It all started from the first moment when I picked her up. I opened the car door for her and said, "You can sit in there if you like". She looked at me a bit funny and said, "Thank you, but I'll wait until we get to a public convenience". I tried to make conversation on the way up to the hinterland and it was very difficult. I tried talking about music and said I like a bit of Debussy and she giggled at me and said, "I bet you do, but you're not getting any today, you cheeky boy". I talked about rock climbing and told her she needed good boots and she giggled again and thought I said she needed a good root. I didn't dare tell her I liked shooting ducks.

'This went on all bloody day so I tried to keep the conversation down to a minimum. I showed her the various plants you could use for bush tucker but I won't even go into the mis-understandings that caused. When we finally climbed up the mountain, we came to this nice clearing next to a cliff, and I unpacked the picnic lunch I'd made, and got the awning, poles and guy ropes out of my pack and put it up to give us a bit of shade. It was getting a bit hot so, without thinking, I stupidly took off my shirt to cool down a bit.

'After lunch, I packed up the gear. As I went to take down the awning I held out the guy rope I'd used to stabilise the canvas and said, "Would you like to dump this over there or tie it under the tree?" She obviously hadn't heard me so I just got on and finished the job. I got the awning down and turned around and I was so shocked I couldn't speak for a minute. There she was, stark naked, lying flat on her back with her legs in the air, and I can tell you, it wasn't the prettiest sight I've seen in my life. It was like staring down into the Carnarvon Gorge. I finally got my voice back and screamed at her, "What the hell are you doing?"

'She looked up at me from between her legs and said, "I was just making up my mind about what you said".

'"What are you talking about, you silly bitch?" I screamed, and held out the guy rope. "I just asked you if you'd like to dump this over there, or tie it under the tree!"

'"Oh, silly me," she said. "I thought you said would I like a hump over there, or die under the trees. I'm so sorry; I'm such a vain old thing. Next time I'll wear my hearing aid."

Estelle was completely thunderstruck and couldn't say a word.

'So, oh what the fuck, I thought, so I dropped me shorts and gave her one, then and there on the spot to shut her up. I'm sorry, Ms Twigden, I know it's against the rules, but what else could I do? She wasn't much good either, so I wouldn't charge her for it.'

That afternoon, Gladys came into the office, full of smiles. Estelle could hardly face her but wasn't in a position to do anything else.

'I just had to come in and thank you, and tell you what a wonderful day we had out bushwalking. It was sooo romantic,' she enthused. 'You were right about Alexander, he was wonderful, so attentive. He really is "Alexander the Great".' She smiled in remembrance. 'I felt just like Deborah Kerr with Stewart Granger in *The Snows of Kilimanjaro*.

Estelle thought it sounded more like Rita Hayworth in *Sadie Thompson*, or Marlon Brando in *Last Tango in Paris*, but didn't voice her opinion.

'I only have one little thing I should mention,' said Gladys, as Estelle waited breathlessly in anticipation. 'His language is a little bit rough, but I suppose, with his background, it's only to be expected, isn't it? But on the whole, I was so pleased that I'd like to leave a little tip

116

for Alexander.' She fished around in her purse and drew out two one-hundred-dollar bills and laid them on the table. 'You will make sure he gets it, won't you?'

'Of course,' said Estelle calmly. 'It sounds like he really deserves it.'

'Oh, he did, Ms Twigden, he really did.'

Chapter 16

They were having their weekly staff meeting in the conference room. Estelle, as usual, had baked a special batch of 'sweet treats,' as she called them; this time it was a batch of cream-filled lamingtons for morning tea. Charles had not as yet discovered this national dish and was mightily impressed. As he chomped his way through his third 'lammie', Estelle mentioned an idea that was dear to her heart.

'I've been going through the booking inquiries and there has been considerable interest in ballroom dancing. I checked the biogs and we have quite a few escorts who included that as an interest. I think we should hire a professional dance trainer to come in and give anyone who's interested a few brush-up classes.'

'That sounds an excellent idea, Estelle,' said Aubrey. 'What are the thoughts of the rest of the panel?'

Both Charles and Penny agreed.

'I was also thinking,' continued Estelle, 'we could use the rooftop terrace that the residents use as their clubhouse. It has a lovely wooden floor and a large undercover area, power points, tables and chairs, which we could move aside, and it would be lovely and cool up there as well.'

'Sounds ideal,' said Aubrey. 'We might also be able to hold other classes up there as well: you know, art

118

classes, Tai Chi, aerobics, heart exercise classes, nothing too strenuous, maybe clay modelling, craft …'

'Craft?' cut in Charles. 'You mean Can't Remember A Fucking Thing classes? I think most of them already have a degree in that.' He chortled away at the old gag while the others looked on disapprovingly.

'Well, shall Penny and I get on to sourcing suitable teachers?' Estelle asked, completely ignoring Charles' interjection.

'An excellent idea, Estelle, it's nice to see these new incentives coming along to help the old folk,' Charles said enthusiastically.

'I don't think we should refer to them as "old folk", Mr Charles, some of them are younger than some of us sitting at this table,' she remarked, looking pointedly at Charles.

'Any other business?' asked Aubrey hastily, trying to deflect any possible retaliation from his partner.

'A new booking,' said Penny, 'a day cruise and fishing excursion on a private yacht for "Adriana".'

'Which one's Adriana?' asked Charles.

'Audrey,' replied Estelle.

'Oh, of course, she's the sixty-year-old ex-air hostess. Nice type, married to a pilot, divorced, no children, in apartment three. Who's the client?'

'A Mr Charlton,' said Penny. 'He's a retired businessman, very well off, owns his own yacht. He has an old business friend out visiting from Japan for a week, a Mr Watanabe, who's very old, but quite fit and strong and loves fishing. Mr Charlton has invited him out on his yacht for a cruise and a day's fishing, and thought it would be nice to take along a companion for his friend. He got our name from our brochure at the Convention Centre. Adriana speaks fluent Japanese so I thought she'd be ideal.'

'What a treasure trove of talent we have at our disposal,' exclaimed Aubrey.

'And nice to see we're picking up business from the brochures too,' said Charles.

Estelle and Penny set to work sourcing out possible coaches for the various classes they'd discussed and Charles suddenly came bursting into their office saying he'd just remembered meeting a lady in one of the clubs he visited regularly, who was a choreographer, and had told him she was looking for work.

'But do you think we need a choreographer, Mr Charles? I was thinking more of a retired ballroom dancer – you know, somebody who could give the escorts a hand with the Schottische, or the Jazz Waltz, Pride of Erin, Fox Trot, Quickstep, or Barn Dance.'

Charles sighed loudly, and said patiently to the uninitiated, 'Valmae is an experienced choreographer, Estelle. She'd know everything about dancing, and how to get a really professional edge to the old dears. I've got her number; I'll give her a ring.' And with that he hurried back into his office.

'Whatever you say, Mr Charles,' sighed Estelle.

Penny and Estelle set about finding other tutors for the intended classes and soon had a list of possible contenders.

Penny started printing up large cards for the escorts, informing them of the various classes that would be available to them, which she would put up on the tenants' notice board, and send copies out to the other escorts. She was so busy, she switched the phone lines directly through to Charles' office.

In the early afternoon, Charles suddenly exploded from his office screaming, 'That stupid, fucking nut-case of a Nip!'

Both Estelle and Penny looked up startled.

'What's happened, Charlie, er, Mr Charles?'

'That fucking wacky Watanabe wanker, that's what happened,' screamed Charles, which brought Aubrey rushing from his office, with a mouthful of leftover lamington oozing from the corner of his mouth.

'He's harpooned a fucking whale!' screamed Charles.

'What?' said Aubrey, spitting crumbs and bits of chocolate icing and coconut everywhere.

'I've had the fucking water police on one phone, and fucking Greenpeace on the other, and fucking Sea World on my mobile! There's absolute fucking mayhem!'

'Now, calm down, Charles,' said Aubrey, wiping his mouth with his handkerchief, 'and tell us exactly what has happened.'

'And please watch your language, Mr Charles,' said Estelle in a reprimanding tone. 'There's a young lady present.'

121

Charles took a deep breath to regain control and said, 'Mr Whirlgig Watanabe, who has obviously got a kink in his kimono, was sitting in the saloon, having his morning pint of sake, and admiring an old harpoon hanging on the wall, which the owner had hung there for a decorative, nautical effect, when he heard someone on deck yelling, "Whales! – Whales! – Look at the whales!" The nutty Nip, no doubt responding to some long-hidden primitive urge, went totally berserk, grabbed the harpoon off the wall, ran out on deck, tied it to one of the mooring ropes, leant over the rail and let fly at one of the poor sods that breached, or whatever it is they do, right next to the fucking boat!

'The fucking whale took off at a rate of knots, dragging the yacht behind it for miles! Who did he think he was, fucking Captain Ahab?'

'Oh, it wasn't Miggaloo the white whale, was it?' asked Penny in obvious distress.

'How the fuck would I know what colour it was?' screamed Charles.

'Why didn't they cut the rope?' asked Aubrey.

'With a six-inch fishing knife? They were going fishing, not wild whale hunting!'

'They radioed for help,' Charles continued, 'and pretty soon there were police boats and helicopters, Greenpeace, Sea World and probably the entire fucking Australian Navy all over the place!'

'Oh, is the whale all right?' asked Penny, obviously upset.

'How the fucking hell do I know,' screamed Charles.

122

'And how did they get our number?' asked Aubrey.

'Edith or Audrey or bloody Adriana, or whatever her name is, radioed for them to contact us. She thought she should keep us informed!'

A sudden thought hit Charles.

'God,' he said, 'I can just see the headlines: "Elderly Escort Harpooned with Her Pants Down in Whale Drama!" It'll cause a huge International Incident! And we'll be involved!'

'How is Adriana?' asked Penny.

'Oh, she'll be all right,' said Estelle. 'She survived two near plane crashes in Manila.'

'What do we do now?' asked Aubrey.

'Well, the sperm will certainly hit the propeller now,' moaned Charles. 'We'll be a laughing stock.'

'I don't know what all the fuss is about,' said Estelle, calmly. 'An old Japanese gentleman goes fishing and lands a whale. He probably felt like some Sashimi. They're very fond of whale meat, you know.'

Charles looked at her, speechless, groaned, and headed back to his office. Estelle shrugged and went back to work. Aubrey followed Charles back to his office and Penny went to the switchboard to turn the incoming calls back to Reception.

'We'd better take the incoming calls in here,' she said, 'He gets so excited.'

Chapter 17

As it turned out, 'The Whale Episode,' as it was referred to, did attract its fair share of media coverage. But it was not the disaster Charles had predicted; in fact, quite the opposite. There were the inevitable photographs and articles in the newspapers and a few crank calls asking if they could book an escort for whale harpooning, or porpoise pulling, or shark shagging, but on the whole it was fairly positive, with even more people hearing of the escort agency and inquiring about their services, and, more importantly, making bookings. Adriana was still a fairly attractive-looking woman, coming from an age when all air hostesses, or flight attendants as they are now called, were expected to be gorgeous. The photographs of her in the newspapers were flattering and obviously appealing to the older male clients, and she was booked out for months in advance.

Television channels, always desperate for any bit of oddball news to sensationalise, flocked to the agency for interviews and television appearances. *Good Morning Australia* asked for a couple of representatives from the Agency to appear on their programme, and suddenly Charles discovered that any publicity was good publicity. He and Aubrey eagerly agreed to appear on the programme.

They were flown down to Sydney, in economy class, Charles noted testily, to appear on the show and, unexpectedly, Aubrey was terribly excited. On the other hand, Charles was unusually quiet, which was just as well because Aubrey couldn't shut up. He went on about the thrill of appearing on television; did Charles think the suit he'd chosen was suitable for the screen? Did he think they'd have to wear make-up, because he didn't want to look like a big girl? Did he think that television would make him look fatter? He'd heard it did. What questions did he think they'd ask? What angle did he think they should take? Should they go for serious or comedy? On and on he went until Charles was ready to throw him out of the plane.

They had a car waiting for them at the airport that whisked them straight to the television channel and into Wardrobe and Make-up. It was just as well they were made up because by now Aubrey's face had become quite flushed and he looked more like Chief Crazy Horse about to be interviewed on the outcome of the Battle of Little Big Horn. The make-up artists were experts of course and managed to apply pan-cake, several shades lighter than normal, to bring the flush down to 'Lightly sun-tanned'. He continued chatting merrily through Wardrobe and Make-up and into the studio where the floor manager was waiting for them.

Aubrey nodded enthusiastically as the floor manager showed them where they would be sitting, gave a quick run-down on commercial breaks and pointed out the three cameras that would be covering the interview. He realised that Aubrey was a little hyper and did his best to calm him down while Charles seemed to take everything in his stride.

The commercial break prior to their appearance began and they were taken to their places and introduced to the presenters. The presenters, a handsome television type and his very attractive female co-presenter were very friendly and again gave instructions on what was going to happen. Aubrey kept nodding and chatting affably while Charles simply nodded and sat waiting.

The floor manager gave a stand-by call of five seconds to go and pointed to the camera that would be taking the opening shot.

Five, four, three, two, and then he waved his hand to cue the presenter.

'There's been a lot of attention lately,' said the handsome male presenter, 'about a rather unusual escort agency, operating out of the Gold Coast in Queensland. I say "unusual" because this escort agency is a little different from the escort agencies we usually hear about. This agency caters solely for the over fifty-five age bracket. Their brochure and website claim there is definitely no sex involved and the agency is aimed at lonely, elderly, or should I say "mature" clients, who for one reason or another have been separated from their partners, yet still desire company on their outings.

'And to tell us a little bit more about the service, I'd like to introduce Mr Charles Wellington and Mr Aubrey

Acres, who are owners and co-founders of this extraordinary service. Good morning gentlemen.'

The red light on camera two came on and suddenly Aubrey became utterly transfixed and totally mesmerised. His face and mind immediately became blank and he was unable to utter a single word. His jaw went a little slack, which made him look like a dribbling patient in a nursing home for the mentally disabled, and his eyes glazed over like ice on a pond.

Without noticing this, Charles suddenly became a presenter's dream, smiling and gesturing, his face expressive, his manner, charming.

'Thank you, Don, and good morning to all the viewers out there. Yes, I know it sounds a little unusual, but we believe that although we have begun to age a little, there is still a lot of living to do out there. But, as you so rightly said, a lot of us lose our partners or decide to retire to glorious, sunny Queensland. I'm originally a Pommie myself, and I can tell you the Gold Coast has remarkable weather and natural attractions for retirees, as well as the young. And some wonderful pastimes to experience as well, apart from the world famous theme parks – wouldn't you agree, Aubrey?'

But Aubrey was away with the pixies and didn't respond, just sitting there, as if cast in stone and barely breathing.

The female presenter, Delvene, recognising the signs of stage fright and all-out panic, picked up the cue like the experienced pro she was.

'Well, I think it's a marvellous idea, don't you, Don? I mean, the world is so youth conscious nowadays, and why shouldn't the older generation be able to have a bit of fun as well? And, as you say, if they've moved to a strange place and left their friends behind, it must get terribly lonely for them.'

She turned hopefully once again to Aubrey for his response; however, he remained completely catatonic and unable to even close his slack, gaping mouth, which was doing nothing to improve his management image. By now realising the state Aubrey was in, Charles again quickly took up the cudgels.

'Exactly,' said Charles. 'So we recognised the need and set about doing something about it. We auditioned literally hundreds of applicants for our escorts, which, of course, gave us the opportunity to pick and choose and take on only the most suitable.'

'Would they be mostly women?' asked Don.

'No, not at all,' replied Charles, well into his subject. 'We cater for both sexes. Because, after all, loneliness doesn't discriminate, so why should we?'

'So, tell us about the "Whale Experience", as it's been referred to in the press,' encouraged Don, again trying to include Aubrey in the conversation, 'It caused quite a stir, I believe.'

The response from Aubrey was exactly as before: zilch. The blinds were down and not a chink of light was showing through.

'That was an unfortunate occurrence,' Charles jumped in. 'Nothing to do with our escort, of course. She was absolutely unhurt and had a good laugh about it later in hospital – just for observation, of course,' he quickly threw in. 'No, we had an elderly Japanese tourist who wanted a little company while he went out on a yacht and fishing excursion that had been arranged by an Australian friend and, well, things got a little out of hand.'

'He actually harpooned a whale?' laughed Delvene, disbelievingly.

'Well, the Japanese do love their fishing,' Charles laughed back.

Not even a sign of recognition from Aubrey.

'Anyway, it was all cleared up pretty quickly,' said Charles. 'The water police and Sea World were marvellous about it. Greenpeace were a little miffed though.'

'But what about the Japanese gentleman?' Don laughed.

'Oh, I think his tourist visa was cancelled and he was sent back to Nagasaki,' replied Charles.

The interview continued for a few more minutes with Charles being informative and vivacious, and Aubrey remaining in his Near Death Experience. Eventually it was time to move on and make way for the next guest, who happened to be an Australian Country and Western star who had sold a zillion records about the Australian outback, which of course were all sung in a distinctly Memphis American accent. As the show went into its next commercial break, Charles thanked the presenters for having them on the show, they thanked him for appearing, and two stage-hands carried the still comatose Aubrey from the studio.

Remarkably, as soon as Aubrey was returned to make-up, he suddenly recovered, as if nothing had happened, and reverted to his previous bright and chatty self, as though someone had thrown an electric switch to turn him back on, or maybe twisted the knob on the oxygen machine.

'Well, that went well, I think, don't you?' he beamed at Charles.

Disbelievingly, Charles looked him in the eye for a long moment and then smiled and said, 'Aubs, you were perfect.'

'Oh, go on,' Aubrey said bashfully, 'you're just saying that. You were very good too.'

'Oh, thank you, Aubs, there's nothing I appreciate more than a considerate and self-effacing co-star.'

Aubrey was so moved he impulsively stuck out his hand for Charles to shake. Charles smiled and the two friends shook hands warmly. But Aubrey couldn't resist one more assurance.

'Honestly, you really think I was all right?'

'Aubs, you're an absolute natural.'

They flew back to the Gold Coast and were greeted with much excitement and exuberance from Estelle and Penny.

'That was wonderful!' Estelle enthused. 'And it was such good publicity!'

'The phones have been ringing off the hook!' exclaimed Penny. 'You were a hit!'

'Did you tape it?' asked Aubrey, eagerly.

The two women looked at each other, a little embarrassed.

'We tried to,' lied Estelle, 'but the tape machine must've broken down, or I didn't program it properly. I'm useless with these newfangled technical gizmos.'

'Oh, what a pity,' said Aubrey, 'I was so looking forward to seeing it.'

'Anyway,' said Penny, attempting to bring the awkward moment to a close, 'the main thing was, it was great publicity. And you both looked very … handsome,' she said, for the want of a better word.

'Yes, but I wish I could've actually seen it,' groaned Aubrey.

Oh, I don't think so, thought Penny, with a knowing look at Charles.

Chapter 18

The morning of the first dance class, Estelle arrived at the office carrying a large, lumpy, black garbage bag. Penny said, 'What's in the body bag? Don't tell me one of the tenants has carked it.'

'Don't be tasteless, Penny, it's just a bit of insurance.'

Before Penny could inquire further, in walked Valmae, the dance instructor. She was in her late forties, incredibly fit, with bright red hair piled on top of her head in a chignon and wearing full stage makeup that must have been applied with a trowel. 'Morning,' she said brightly as she removed her jacket to reveal a slim curvaceous body in a black leotard and tights. 'Hi, I'm Valmae. Charlie asked me to come in and give your dancers a bit of a workout.'

'Well, hardly a workout,' said Estelle. 'They just need a bit of a brush-up on their dance steps.'

'Right,' said Valmae. 'How many of the little darlings have I got?'

'Well, it's a good turnout,' said Estelle, as she watched Valmae throw her large shoulder bag on another chair, sit down and change her runners for a pair of gold, four-inch heel sandals. 'I'd say there's about twenty.'

Valmae looked up and noticed Estelle's rather puzzled look and said, 'Oh, these are just my work shoes. If you're going to dance in them, you've got to practise in them.'

'They're cool!' said Penny. 'Where could I pick up a pair?'

Before the conversation turned into a discussion on 'tasteless' fashion, Estelle said, 'We're holding the classes on the rooftop terrace. If you'd like to follow me, I'll show you the way and introduce you to everybody.'

'Fair enough,' said Valmae, as she picked up her bag and followed Estelle to the stairs.

All the escorts for the dance class were gathered on the rooftop, almost exclusively dressed in shapeless tracksuits and runners, all different shapes and sizes, chatting and laughing amongst themselves. As soon as Estelle and Valmae entered, a sudden hush descended on the assembly of middle-aged participants.

Cissie-nee-Cheryl, whispered to Bettina-nee-Betty, 'Well, I'd say *she's* had a bit of work done on her.'

With a look that could only be described as snide, Bettina whispered back, 'I'd say a complete replacement job. I'll bet she used to be a stripper.'

'Well, at her age, she'd need more than seven veils now,' replied Cissie bitchily.

The men in the group just stood and stared, some of them trying to remember *why* they were staring.

'Gawd, this is going to be a challenge,' Valmae muttered to herself, and then, brightly, 'Hi, everyone, I'm Valmae.' She used that awful upward inflection at the end of every sentence that almost seems to be a national vocal trait.

Estelle took Valmae around the crowd and introduced her.

Valmae smiled and shook limp-wristed hands and immediately forgot the names. She unpacked her CD player from her capacious handbag and switched it on.

'Right, if everybody would line up, we'll start the class with a few stretching exercises. We don't want to damage any of our muscles or joints, do we?'

'I don't care about me muscles,' said Raoul, nee Fred, 'but I'd hate to damage the joint in me pocket.'

Everybody laughed, except Estelle, of course, who said as she made her way to the stairs, 'Well, I'll leave you to it. Hope you all have a lovely time.'

'Oh, dear, I hope Mr Charles has done the right thing,' she said to Penny as she entered Reception.

'Oh, they'll be fine,' said Penny, reassuringly. 'They'll have a great time.'

Just then a rather good-looking young man entered the office and Penny, thinking he must be a salesman or a business associate of Aubrey's or Charles', gave him the benefit of her most winning smile and said, 'Yes, can I help you?'

The young man returned the smile almost shyly and replied, 'Yes, I'd like to hire an escort – or rather two.'

'You're a bit greedy, aren't you, sonny?' laughed Penny. 'I think you've come to the wrong sort of escort service.'

'No,' said the young man, 'you don't understand, I'm looking for a mother and a father.'

'We're not a missing persons agency either,' said Penny. 'We're an escort agency for the over fifties.'

'I know,' said the young man, 'that's why I thought you might be able to help me out.'

Estelle who had overheard the conversation, said, 'I think you'd better come in and sit down, young man.'

'Thank you,' he said pleasantly as he made his way to Estelle's desk and sat in the chair opposite.

'Now, what's this all about?' she said.

'Well,' said the young man, 'my name is Colin, and I'm engaged to this wonderful, beautiful young lady I met in England, and she's coming out here for a holiday to meet my parents before we return to England to get married.'

'So why do you need to hire a mother and father?

'Well …' Colin looked a little embarrassed, 'that's the problem. I haven't got any. Well, I have, but I've sort of lost them.'

'So why didn't you tell her?' asked Penny.

'Well, she's from a very close family and she thinks family is everything. They all live in the same neighbourhood we'll be living in, and they all spend a lot of time with each other.'

'So, why didn't you just tell her your parents were dead?'

Colin dropped his head, in shame. 'They're not, that's the problem.'

'What do you mean?' asked Estelle.

135

'My mother is a junkie who lives with a bikie boyfriend, and my father's a drunk – well, alcoholic, really. So you see I couldn't introduce her to *them*. She'd never marry me if she found out. She'll only be over here for a week, so I thought if I could hire a nice couple to pretend to be my mother and father for the week, we could then go back to England and get married and she need never see them again.'

Estelle and Penny looked at one another, sympathising with this nice young man's dilemma.

Finally, Estelle said, 'Well, I can't promise anything, but I'll ask around our escorts and see if any of them are willing to take on the job. All of our escorts are single without partners, you see. They won't be living together you realise, so your fiancée wouldn't be able to stay over for the night or anything like that.'

'Oh, that's all right,' Colin said, looking a little more optimistic. 'We could just all go out together; to dinner and tourist places; maybe drives in the country. I just want to make a good impression on her.'

'What happens when she invites them over for the wedding?' asked Penny, foreseeing some future problems.

'Well, they could make some last minute excuse, like, er, one of them can't fly for medical reasons ... or maybe they could both get killed in a plane crash or something,' he said, warming to the idea.

'A bit gruesome, don't you think?' said Estelle. 'And besides, your fiancée would insist on going to the funeral.'

136

'We don't do funerals,' said Penny. 'Well, not as an outing, anyway. That's more of an "inside" job that goes with the territory, depending on who dies.'

'Look, I know there could be a few … complications along the way,' said Colin, 'but I'm sure I could deal with them. I can always just lie. I mean, I'll be a husband by then and all husbands lie to their wives.'

'Well,' said Estelle, a bit taken aback, 'that may not be the best way to start the marriage. As I said, we'll see what we can do, but I'm not making any promises.'

'That's all I'm asking,' Colin smiled gratefully.

'Would you have a picture of yourself so we can see if we can find a couple who could possibly look like you? It might help.'

Colin fished in his wallet and extracted a photograph of himself and his fiancée, and handed it to Estelle.

'And this is your fiancée, I take it?' she said, showing it to Penny, whose eyes widened slightly.

'Yes,' drooled Colin. 'Isn't she gorgeous?'

'Hmmm, lovely complexion,' said Penny, 'beautiful … dark skin.'

Colin smiled proudly. 'Yes. She's Sudanese … African.'

'Well, I'm glad it's *your* parents we're trying to find,' said Penny, 'otherwise we'd be in terrible strife. We're fresh out of bla– Sudanese escorts.'

'She is very beautiful,' said Estelle, agreeably. 'I'm sure you'll be very happy together.'

'And in London,' Penny also tried to be supportive, 'you're the one who's going to stand out.'

Estelle shot her a disapproving look and said to Colin, 'Can you leave this with us? It will give us something to work with.'

'Of course,' he replied. 'I've got at least another hundred at home.'

Penny picked up her notebook and pen. 'Just leave your name, address and phone number and we'll get back to you if we come up with any likely contenders.'

'You make them sound like boxers,' laughed Colin.

'Well, you do want them to behave like they're married, don't you?' replied Penny slyly.

The details completed, Colin thanked them, got up and moved to the front door, as Penny turned to Estelle. 'Well, got any suggestions?'

'I'm thinking about it,' said Estelle, opening her files. 'It's not impossible.'

Later on Estelle decided she should pop in to the dance class to see how things were going. On arriving, she was shocked to see everyone had collapsed on the floor, many writhing in agony and moaning.

'Good heavens! What on earth happened?' she asked incredulously.

'Fuckin' Raoul,' groaned Valmae, writhing in pain and holding her leg, 'that's what fuckin' happened.'

Apparently Raoul had not been joking. When the class asked to break for morning tea after the warm-up stretch session, and a few demonstration steps, Valmae was amazed. They'd only been exercising for about an hour and she couldn't believe they'd need a break so soon. But, the class won out, saying they were exhausted after the high kicks, bumps and grinds and the splits, so out came the English Breakfast and Ginger Nut biscuits and everybody settled down for a nice cuppa. All except Raoul who discreetly disappeared down the back stairs fire escape, to a secluded spot in the garden where he lit up the joint he had indeed secreted in his pocket. Then he remembered he hadn't taken his heart medication and popped one of the pills in his mouth.

Valmae was inwardly seething about Charles. He had asked her if she would drop in and give a few of his old friends some dance classes. She hadn't realised that he literally meant '*old*' friends! What the hell was she supposed to accomplish?

She didn't think they'd be up to the Salsa, Tango, American Tribal Fusion or especially Hip Hop, so she chatted with a few of the class during tea break and discovered that they had expected a brush-up on their Ballroom steps, which, of course, Charles hadn't mentioned. She was a professional choreographer! What the fuck did she know about Ballroom dancing? Still, being a pro, which Veronique-nee-Vera had suspected all along, and had given that opinion, unequivocally, to Magda-nee-Margaret, Valmae had accepted the fee and was damn sure she was going to earn it. The only music she'd brought was modern; the sort of dance music you'd do at nightclubs or cabaret. 'Improvise, Valmae,' she told herself. 'Improvise.'

About twenty minutes later, Valmae clapped her hands and said, in a rather unnecessarily loud and desperate voice, 'All right class, back to work.'

There was the inevitable mumbling of discontent, but cups and saucers were set aside and the dancers returned to the floor.

Valmae demonstrated a short selection of steps and moves, which would've been more appropriate for the chorus line of a Broadway Musical or Kings Cross Drag Club, and said, 'Okay, let's try that, shall we?'

The class looked at each other like this red-headed woman was quite mad, but to their credit they did try, with varying degrees of failure, that caused poor Valmae to wince painfully.

'Right, I'll now show you a few steps that may come in handy.' She demonstrated the Feather Step, Chain Turns and the Gancho, and then encouraged them to try them with each other.

At this point Raoul hit the floor with all the confidence and aplomb of a Rudolph Nureyev on speed and cheap generic steroids, twisting, sliding, hip dropping (which certainly wasn't good with his replacement), changing partners, and twirling them across the floor with such vigour that some of the ladies crashed into the wall. After all, he had seen the film *Strictly Ballroom* five times and remembered the steps off by heart.

However, he did not take into account that the dancers in the film were experienced, younger and a whole lot more agile and certainly more flexible. In his exuberance, he grabbed Valmae and spun her around the floor, twirling dangerously close to the other couples, who were intent on looking at their feet, counting the beats and deeply concentrating on their steps. Inevitably, disastrous collisions occurred, which brought to mind the car chase sequence in *The Blues Brothers*.

The result was catastrophic. Bodies lay scattered all over the floor culminating in a twisted, screaming pile, heaped on top of each other, in the middle of the dance floor. And underneath this writhing heap lay a screaming Valmae, her face contorted in pain.

And it was at this point that Estelle stuck her head through the doorway, checking up on their progress. She froze, horrified at the sight that confronted her, then ran to the writhing mob and began pulling bodies apart from each other and helping them to stand. Valmae was screaming, 'My leg is broken, my fucking leg is broken!'

After freeing Alexander, who, with his invaluable strength gained from wrestling crocodiles and wild buffalo, took control of the disentanglement, Estelle rang through on the house extension and asked Penny to phone for an ambulance for Valmae.

Later, after the ambulance attendants had confirmed that Valmae had not in fact suffered a broken leg, but only a sprain, and was sent home to recuperate, things returned to almost normal. Estelle suggested the class settle down and make another cup of tea, and said she would be back in a few minutes. Raoul, to everybody's relief, had calmed down considerably and become almost chastened. Luckily no serious injuries had been sustained and soon the whole class was laughing and joking about the incident as they righted the furniture and swept up the broken crockery and crushed Ginger Nuts.

Suddenly, through the door swept Estelle, looking like a vision from a Dior nightmare. She was wearing a pale pink creation, the exploding skirt of which was of stiffened tulle and feathers that reached almost to her ankles, and contained more than enough gauze to make at least a hundred mosquito nets for the natives of New Guinea. The top, with a dangerously low neckline, was of embroidered white satin with pink diamante appliqués, and two string glitter straps over her scrawny shoulders, which thankfully stopped it from dropping to her waist. To complete the ensemble she wore her usual sensible black, flat shoes.

The class stood astonished at this unbelievable apparition and stared in hushed disbelief.

'Just a little old thing I used to wear in my ballroom dancing days,' Estelle said, demurely, referring to the dress. 'Now then everyone, take your partners for the Pride of Erin.'

Chapter 19

It wasn't easy finding a suitable mother and father for Colin. Most of the escorts had conflicting engagements and some who had been approached refused because it would mean being tied up for a whole week and possibly missing the Bingo evening. Gisella-nee-Gloria, flatly refused when she discovered the fiancée was a Sudanese.

'Not that I'm a racist,' she'd said. 'It's just that I'd have to try and dissuade my son from an interracial marriage because of the children … No, I'd have to say something,' she muttered as she shook her head. 'I wouldn't be able to help meself.'

And Renaldo-nee-Russell said, 'No, I don't think I'd be any good. I was a lousy father to me own kids and they won't even talk to me. So we'd probably finish up in a god-awful row or even a punch-up, like what happened every Christmas, and I don't think that would impress his fiancée.'

While Estelle and Penny were going through the files one morning, and discussing possible contenders with Aubrey, Charles arrived at work and exploded into reception, terribly excited.

'It's happened! Guess who is going to be a free man soon?'

'*What's* happened?' asked Aubrey.

'That television appearance we did was picked up by the BBC and Lady Celia saw it! It looked obvious to her that I was going to be staying here for a long time, and she began to wonder if I'd ever be going back to England. So, she got in touch with Daddy and he was furious. But, as luck would have it, she'd fallen in love with a Sumo wrestler, and he's proposed! Apparently he was delighted to find someone bigger than he was as a sparring partner and referred to her as his Huge Mummy. She calls him her Little Sparrow! Lord Swindon sent me a letter giving me all the grisly details and, get this, he's offering me a pile of money if I'd consider divorcing his little girl! Consider, is he joking? – Consider? – Would a drowning man refuse a life-raft made of hundred pound notes? I'll jump at the chance!

'Huge Mummy and Little Sparrow want to marry and live in Japan! Lord Swindon is virtually begging me for the divorce because then, Lady Celia will be completely out of the country and out of what little hair he's got left. He's even got connections with the Defence Department and talked them into allowing Lady Celia to sail to Japan on one of their aircraft carriers! Mind you, they'll have to sail with a couple of jet fighter planes short, to lessen the load and make room for her, but he managed it. That is what is called The Power of the Peerage.'

'That's wonderful, Charles,' Aubrey said. 'I mean if that's what you really want. After all, marriage is a commitment.'

'I have been committed, for years: Committed to a loveless marriage, in an insane asylum. No, I couldn't be happier.'

'That television interview must've created quite a stir,' said Penny. 'My Uncle George in London – you know the one I told you about that first day we met on the beach,' she reminded Charles. 'Well, he must've seen it too, and rang my mum because he knew I was out here and living on the Gold Coast. She told him all about me working for you and to cut a long story short he said he was thinking about coming out here for a business trip anyway, so he might drop in and see me.'

'What did you say he did?' asked Charles.

'Import and export, Mum said.'

'Well, that'll be nice for you, dear,' said Estelle, 'catching up with family.'

'I don't know much about him,' said Penny, 'I've only met him a couple of times. He's probably old and boring … Oops, sorry folks, present company excluded.'

The others, by now used to Penny, didn't take offence.

'You don't think he'd like to take on the job of Colin's father, do you?' said Estelle jokingly. 'We're really getting desperate.'

'What about the new ones,' suggested Charles. 'Delilah-nee-Delma, and Joshua-nee-Joe? They both live in the apartments, even though they're on separate floors, and we haven't had any demand for either of them. They might jump at the chance.'

Estelle got the files and photos out of the cabinet and they all scrutinised them and compared them with the photo of Colin.

'These are two that you interviewed, aren't they, Aubs?' Charles said meaningfully.

Aubrey had the good grace to blush and mumbled, 'We might get away with it.'

'But Joshua's got red hair and brown eyes,' said Estelle, 'and Colin's a brunette with blue eyes.'

'Colin could be a throwback,' said Aubrey. 'What's Delilah's colouring?'

'Grey,' replied Estelle, 'with pink eyes.'

'Well, give her a colour rinse, Penny, turn her into a grey-streaked brunette,' suggested Charles, 'and get her a pair of blue contact lenses.'

'Their age group could be all right,' said Estelle, studying the photos more closely. 'I'll go and have a talk with both of them and get their reaction. Pity about Joshua's limp.'

'It'll engender more sympathy,' said Charles. 'He could say it was an old whore wound.'

'War wound! ... Mr Charles!' Estelle sucked her teeth again, as was her habit.

'A lot of war wounds are whore wounds,' said Charles. 'I can remember Dicky Doyle, from the Fusiliers, got a terrible dose of the clap in Seoul on R & R. It ate away his left foot.'

Luckily Estelle didn't hear this as she was on her way to visit Delilah and Joshua in the apartments.

'Oh, I don't know,' said Delilah as she finished her laundry in between checking a cake in the oven, dusting the already shining coffee table, and rearranging the chintz curtains, 'I don't think I'm the motherly type.'

'Don't be silly, you'd be perfect,' said Estelle, 'and you *are* available?'

'Oh, yes, I'd be available, but I don't know. You see,' she drew closer to Estelle and whispered, as tears gathered in her eyes, 'I didn't have any children. I couldn't breastfeed.'

'Colin's twenty-eight years old, I don't think that's a problem. All you have to do is *pretend* to be his mother for a week and make a good impression on his fiancée. At the end of the week, they'll both return to England and you won't have to see them again.'

'You mean I won't be invited to the wedding?' Delilah said, utterly shocked.

'It'll be in England,' explained Estelle. 'You won't be expected to fly over there.'

'But I've got this lovely dress that would be perfect,' complained Delilah. 'Mauve and pink floral, and the hat and bag to match. I'd have to get new shoes though.'

'It's going to be a private ceremony,' lied Estelle, 'no family or friends. A civil ceremony.'

'Oh, that's so sad,' sighed Delilah, almost brought to tears again. 'Oh well, in that case we'll have to make sure we give them a good time while they're out here. I'll have to think of a nice wedding present. Maybe I could crochet something.'

'That would be lovely,' said Estelle, 'So, you'll do it?'

147

'Well, of course! I couldn't let my boy down now, could I? He'd never forgive me.'

One down and one to go, thought Estelle, as she rang Joshua's doorbell.

'G'day, Estelle,' said Joshua, as he opened the door, 'What's up? … I am sorry about my dog crappin' in the pool, but I did scoop it up with me tennis racquet, honest.'

'I know, Joshua, but I'd prefer it if you didn't put it in the geranium pot. It doesn't look nice. Gavin, the gardener-handyman, complains. But that's not what I came to see you about. Can I come in for a minute to discuss it with you?'

Reluctantly Gavin opened the door wider to let Estelle enter and showed her into his living room.

'Sorry about the bit of a mess,' he said, brushing dog hair off the couch. 'I was just cleaning up.'

'That's all right, Joshua,' Estelle said, a little disapprovingly, also noticing a chewed sock, tennis ball and a decimated pair of Y-fronts lying on the floor. 'I'm actually here to offer you an engagement.'

'Oh, thanks, Estelle,' he said almost shyly, 'I know I've sort of got something that appeals to the ladies, but I'm not really the marrying kind.'

It took a moment for Estelle to realise what she'd said, and when she did, she shuddered and continued, ignoring his misunderstanding.

She showed him the photograph of Colin and Lilly, and explained the assignment to him as he sat and listened attentively, while Fritzie, his pure-bred black

148

and white mongrel dog occupied himself humping one of the chewed vinyl chairs on the deck.

Looking at the photo Joshua said, 'What's his name again?'

'Colin,' Estelle replied.

'He looks like a spaniel I used to have, but his name was Frosty.' He thought about the proposition for a while. 'I don't know, Estelle,' he said finally. 'I wouldn't know how to act as a father. I only know about dogs. I used to breed them, y'know.'

'Well, it's exactly the same,' Estelle pounced at the opportunity.

'You mean I'd have to take him for a run every morning and a swim in the surf, and throw a ball for him?'

'I don't see why not,' she replied. 'All four of you could go.'

'Five,' he corrected her. 'Fritzie would have to come too.'

'Right, five,' said Estelle, a little exasperated. 'So you would be interested?'

'Well, I haven't been asked to do one of these escort jobs yet, so I suppose I should wash me feet and give it a go.'

There was another slight, thoughtful pause before he added, 'But I wouldn't have to, you know, move in with this – Delilah, would I? I mean, I wouldn't have to, you know, *sleep* with her?'

'Oh, no, definitely not, Joshua,' she hastily reassured him.

'That's all right then. Because, you know, Fritzie takes up a lot of room … And I don't want anyone getting, you know, jealous.'

'Delilah, or Fritzie?

'Fritzie.'

'Oh, of course. No, he'd have no competition on that score, I can assure you.'

'And I wouldn't have to brush and groom him?'

'Who?'

'This other son of mine,'

'Colin? No, he's old enough to look after himself.'

'And I wouldn't have to, you know, scoop up after him?'

'Colin's a young man, Joshua, not a dog.'

'But you said it'd be the same.'

'Not quite. You'll just have to take him and his fiancée to the beach and a few tourist spots and maybe out to dinner.'

'They don't allow dogs, I've tried.'

Estelle was fast becoming convinced this was all a horrible mistake, but what was she to do?

'When we go to dinner, does he like his kangaroo cooked or raw?' asked Joshua.

Estelle couldn't answer that one so she prepared to leave. 'Well, Joshua, I'll be in touch with the details, and don't worry, I'm sure everything will work out just fine'.

As the door was closing behind her she heard Joshua say, presumably to Fritzie, 'Wonder why she keeps calling me Joshua.'

Chapter 20

Estelle returned to the office a little downhearted about Joshua, but there just didn't seem to be any other man available. She explained to the others what had happened with Delilah and Joshua, and voiced her premonition of impending doom if they put the two of them together. She supposed Colin's 'father' could perhaps suddenly die just before Lilly arrived but that would leave the couple stuck with Delilah for the whole time and the Sudanese fiancée could end up massacring Delilah out of sheer frustration. She had heard the Sudanese could be very volatile. And if that happened it could put a real dampener on the wedding.

The others dismissed her concerns and were mainly relieved that they'd at last found a couple to fill the assignment and tried to assure her that everything would be fine. Charles offered to 'train' the soon-to-be parents in the art of social graces and correct behaviour, but Estelle, remembering what had happened with the dance class choreographer he'd organised, immediately stepped in and declined the offer, saying, thanks all the same, Mr Charles, but she thought perhaps she and Penny should take on the job.

Estelle and Penny discussed their war plan and set about arranging suitable times for all concerned. They would begin by working individually with each of the 'parents' and, when they thought it appropriate, they would bring mother, father and son together for the final training. They had a week before Colin's fiancée arrived, which they hoped would be enough time.

Estelle's first session with Delilah was a little stressful, but not impossible. As per plan, both Delilah and Joshua had been presented with a large blow-up photo of Colin and his fiancée, Lilly, and instructed to hang the picture on a wall and to look at it as much as possible to acquaint themselves with the couple and hopefully, develop a closeness and bond with them. This was going to be a trial for Delilah because she tended to break into tears every time she looked at the photograph of her 'son'. Whilst drying her eyes and blowing her nose with her lace-edged handkerchief, she listened as Estelle attempted to discuss the overall plan with her and she immediately went into another flood of tears, bemoaning the fact that she never had the chance to have real children of her own. This wasn't solely because of her breastfeeding problem, but the main obstacle was that nobody had ever actually asked her for a tumble, or had even tried to force themselves upon her.

Estelle looked at her more closely and understood why. Delilah was a little round lady. She had a little voice, a round face, little pink eyes, round glasses, little feet, round body, little hands and a round head of fluffy grey hair, and had obviously been 'round very little, sexually. If the country was invaded she would never have been raped by the marauding soldiers, she would've been too occupied darning their socks, mending their uniforms, cooking their meals and polishing their bayonets.

If there was a small problem, it was that Delilah was all together *too* motherly; in fact, she was smotherly. Estelle couldn't imagine any man looking at her as anything but his mother. Obviously Aubrey had interviewed and accepted her as a tenant. It was no wonder she hadn't had any escort work. But in this case it could be a definite bonus if only they could tone her down a bit. Otherwise, Colin and Lilly wouldn't be able to wait to escape back to England or anywhere.

On the other hand, Penny was having a larger problem with Joshua. He was gauche, ordinary looking, tall and thin with a large nose and ears, and sparse reddish-coloured hair that completely evaporated on the top of his skull but flourished out of his nose and ears.

His conversation consisted entirely of canine capers. No matter how hard Penny tried to find the man inside, his replies always seemed to return to his dog, Fritzie, or the dogs he used to train before he retired, their individual personalities and traits, and their sometimes peculiar breeding habits. But somehow, Penny sensed a mystery deep inside the man. How to release that inner man and turn him into the fatherly type? That was the question.

She was quite wrong really. There was no inner mystery to Joshua. What you saw was what you got: a plain, old, ordinary man with the brain of a border collie.

'For God's sake, they're only supposed to be elderly parents; we're not looking for a Tom Hanks and a Britney Spears!' shouted Charles. 'They just have to look and act normal!'

'Yes, well, *that* is the problem,' said Penny.

'Young Colin is asking us to find two lovely elderly people he can be proud of, to impress his fiancée,' said Estelle, patiently. 'We just need a little time. Penny and I have got a few ideas that just may work.'

'We don't have a year, Estelle,' sighed Charles, 'we only have a week. Just dress them up and tell them to keep their mouths shut for a few days. They don't even have to talk to each other; in fact, that would be even more realistic for a couple who are supposed to have been married for forty years.'

Penny ignored him and turned once again to Estelle.

'We can dress them up but that's not going to be enough. We want them to be a lovable and loving couple – the perfect Mum and Dad.'

Charles groaned and returned to his office.

'They hardly know one another,' said Estelle to Penny. 'I think we should try to bring them closer together, as a couple. We'll watch how they react. I'm sure Delilah will be fine but Joshua could be a problem. He won't go anywhere without Fritzie.'

'How about we get them together over coffee somewhere?' Penny suggested, 'just so they can get to know each other.'

'Good idea,' said Estelle. 'I'll check it out with them.'

It didn't quite work out as planned. Delilah offered to prepare a nice morning tea for them all in her apartment, rather than go out to one of those awful modern cafes, which Estelle and Penny thought an excellent idea. Joshua reluctantly agreed, on the condition that Fritzie was also invited. Estelle and Penny didn't see this as a problem as long as Fritzie was restrained on a leash.

On the arranged morning, Penny and Estelle arrived first and were terribly impressed with the table arrangement – 'terribly' being the operative word. It was all totally over the top and ladylike: delicate Royal Doulton fine bone china tea set, with teapot and strainer, in an all-over pattern of pale pink rosebuds on a white background; fine, lace-edged, white linen tablecloth, with yet more pink rosebuds and matching lace-edged linen serviettes; a diamond-cut crystal rose bowl complete with a fresh pink rosebud arrangement; tiny silver cutlery and servers, with a pink rosebud motif on the handles. Everything matched the white linen seat covers with, of course, pale pink rosebud appliqués.

It was all so delicate and formal, there would be no opportunity to relax and enjoy the tea party and get to know each other for fear of breaking the crockery or spilling a drop of Earl Grey tea on the cloth, or wiping your lipstick on the serviette. Estelle and Penny felt they should don white gloves, with of course, a pale pink rosebud pattern, before they sat down.

Joshua arrived with Fritzie, on his leash as he'd promised Estelle, looking like a stock hand and his dog

155

just arrived back from a particularly hard month in the desert, droving cattle. The contrast was palpable.

At that particular point in time, Delilah was setting out the repast for her guests: delicately decorated little cakes and pastries; cucumber sandwiches; and a large, beautifully decorated cream sponge, which she had made earlier in the morning. She had arisen from her bed at dawn, in order to vacuum and polish the already spotless apartment. She was now bending down at the oven removing a tray of dainty savouries she'd had warming for her guests.

The actual sequence of events that followed, nobody later could quite remember, even if they wanted to.

Joshua stepped into the room and came to an abrupt stop, his eyes and jaw opened in amazement at the all-too-feminine vista before him. Such was his surprise that he dropped the leash restraining the over-exuberant Fritzie, who immediately lunged forward to greet the assembled party, and in his excitement, flew around the room dragging the leash behind him like a lethal lasso. The tea table was the first to go, with a disastrous crash, quickly followed by the smashing of crockery, cutlery, and the various plates of delicacies flying through the air, spattering the curtains, walls and furniture, and plummeting to the floor. The screaming, falling, air-clutching Estelle and Penny, tripped by the lethal leash, brought up the rear, in a breathtaking catastrophe of horrific proportions.

Before the bending Delilah had the time to react to the carnage, Fritzie spied her out of the corner of his

156

eye and, never a canine to miss an opportunity, leaped straight onto her rear end and started humping her. Delilah's shocked response, thinking she was being sexually attacked by Joshua, caused her to scream loudly and grab the first weapon to hand, which happened to be her largest cast-iron skillet. She spun around, remarkably quickly for her age, and lashed out at her attacker. Unfortunately, or fortunately, depending on your viewpoint, Joshua had responded to the disaster swiftly, and thrown himself at Fritzie in order to restrain him from the indignity of being accused of being a would-be rapist, thus bringing himself directly into the trajectory of the swinging skillet. The skillet made a crushing impact with his head and laid him out cold, while Fritzie whimpered and retreated back out the still-open front door, dragging the leash, and a dining chair, behind him.

Still screaming and by now hysterical, Delilah bent over the prone body of Joshua, emitting even louder Greek-like funeral wailing, out of fear she had killed him. Estelle and Penny extricated themselves from the debris and, wiping whipped cream, sponge cake, tea and milk from their faces and attire, ran to comfort her, to little avail.

Neighbours from the adjacent apartments materialised through the door, no doubt alerted by the cacophony, jabbering and pointing like a crowd of bystanders at a fatal car crash, and for the moment doing nothing to assist, except the few who were eagerly picking up squashed bits of cake and scones and stuffing them into their mouths as they surveyed the chaos.

Finally, Estelle and Penny were able to get Delilah back under control by confirming that Joshua was indeed only unconscious and unlikely to sustain any lasting damage. The neighbours, having their offers of help politely but firmly declined, retreated reluctantly to their own apartments with much eager discussion amongst themselves over the dramatic incident.

Delilah was deposited on the couch and given a cup of hot tea and a cucumber sandwich from the floor to help her recover.

Estelle and Penny stood surveying the catastrophic scene for a few moments before Penny observed, 'Well, this puts a bit of a dampener on the ideal Darby and Joan booking.'

Chapter 21

'We've got to get a few more new escorts,' said Estelle, decisively, to Charles and Aubrey.

'Well, put another advertisement in the papers,' replied Charles.

'We don't need to, we've got a list of people waiting to be interviewed. It's just that you and Mr Aubrey have been so busy.'

'Well, can't you and Penny do it? You both know by now the types that are in demand.' Charles looked at Aubrey, meaningfully. 'And we certainly *don't* need another Delilah or Joshua!'

'It's such a shame about them,' Penny said. 'I thought they had potential, with a bit of training.'

'Potential? Training?' roared Charles. 'Potential for disaster, and training with a chair and a whip. And that dog has to be put into a kennel. And I don't mean bloody Fritzie.'

'How is Joshua, by the way?' asked Aubrey.

'He had to go into hospital for observation,' said Estelle, 'but they stitched him up and sent him home. He seems to be recovering.'

'And what about poor Delilah?'

'She seems to be over most of the shock. She's been heavily into therapy.'

'Psychiatry?' asked Aubrey.

'No, housework. She had so much cleaning up, painting and repairing to do after the, er, incident, she's almost back to her old, sterile self.'

'That's nice, the dear old thing,' smiled Aubrey, a little consoled.

'So it's okay for ET and me to do some auditioning?' asked Penny.

'I,' groaned Charles.

'Me,' Estelle contradicted him.

'Oh, all right, you too.' And off he stomped to his office.

'What do we do about poor Colin?' asked Estelle. 'He'll be so disappointed.'

'Well, it's too late to get anybody else, even if there was somebody,' said Penny, 'so I've been thinking ...' She turned to Aubrey. 'What about you and Estelle?'

Estelle and Aubrey looked at each other in shock. 'Us?' they said, almost in unison.

'Well, why not? You'd make a perfect old married couple. You're both nice people, loving, caring, and you're not all that weird looking, and even more importantly, you'd both be cheap.'

'But – but – but ...' Aubrey spluttered, while Estelle went into blushing mode and hung her head.

'Well, why don't you both just think about it?' said Penny. 'Now, I'm going to pop out and leave you two old lovebirds together to make up your mind.' And with a devious grin, she picked up her handbag and left.

For a moment, Estelle and Aubrey couldn't even bring themselves to look at each other. Aubrey crashed straight back to puberty, embarrassed and shyly kicking his foot against the carpet, and suddenly not sure of what to do with his hands. Estelle sat stock still, staring straight ahead.

Eventually, she returned to her business-like self again and said, 'I suppose it's possible. I mean there's no reason why we couldn't do it. I mean, it would help Colin, wouldn't it? And, I mean, it would be cheaper for the company, wouldn't it? I mean …' Her voice trailed off to a stop as she looked up at Aubrey and their eyes locked.

'Well,' said Aubrey, uncertainly. 'I suppose we could get away with it. I mean, if you'd want to. I mean, after all, it is only business. I mean, isn't it?'

'Let's do it,' said Estelle decisively. 'Anyway, it could be fun.'

'Right! Let's,' said Aubrey and fled to the sanctuary of his office.

'I'll call Colin and ask him in to see if he approves, shall I?' she called after him. 'And I'll ask him to come in for a chat.'

'Right, good idea,' called Aubrey, as he disappeared.

Colin couldn't have been happier. He hadn't met Aubrey before and he was most impressed: so mature, so sensible, so pleasant, so respectable. In his mind he couldn't help comparing Aubrey to his real father and the comparison was more than favourable. Estelle was a little more reserved but still a lovely lady and one he would be proud to call his mother. She even looked a bit

161

like him, he thought; the same sort of soulful eyes, the thin straight nose, the slight stubble on her chin. No, she'd be perfect.

They chatted together for an hour, and got to know a lot about each other, and by the time Colin left, all the arrangements had been made for Estelle and Aubrey's week of proud parenthood with their loving son and future daughter-in-law. They would meet up at the airport to welcome Lilly, Aubrey would drive them all to the hotel where they would be staying, they'd have a drink, or maybe a cup of tea for Estelle, just to be on the safe side, and make arrangements to meet up the next day for an outing, giving the young lovebirds an evening alone to catch up on each other's news, and probably a lot of bonking.

The big day arrived and Aubrey drove to Estelle's house to pick her up for the meeting with Colin at the airport.

Aubrey knocked on the door and a moment later the door opened to reveal a completely new Estelle. Aubrey stood, open mouthed and astonished. This had not been a simple make-over, this had been a complete renovation job.

She was beautifully dressed in a well-tailored, navy blue slacks suit, and a soft white blouse with a flattering ruffle at the throat. He didn't get to notice if she was still wearing the usual flat black court shoes because he could hardly take his eyes off her face and hair. Her hair had been rinsed in an auburn shade and styled in soft flattering waves that curled around her face and over

162

her ears leaving enough of her lobes exposed to reveal delicate gold earrings, inlaid with a couple of tiny diamonds. Her face had been made up to perfection: her skin seemed much softer, her complexion flawless and the stubble had obviously been removed by electrolysis. The horn-rimmed glasses had disappeared and her eyebrows had been shaped perfectly and her eyelids slightly tinted to highlight her dark brown mascara-lined, now contact-lensed eyes that, at the moment, sparkled like sunlight on a cesspool. Her lips suggested a touch of Botox, but just enough to make them visible, and they were rouged with a subtle coral shade of lipstick.

To Aubrey, the effect was literally stunning.

Penny stepped up from behind Estelle and said, 'What do you reckon, not bad, eh?'

Not bad? Aubrey thought. My God, she's almost beautiful!

But instead he said, 'Ms Twigdon, I think you've been hiding your light under a bushel. You look very nice.'

'Why, thank you, Mr Aubrey. It's all been Penny's work. Isn't she marvellous?'

'Well done, Penny,' he said. 'I think you're due for a raise. And if you can do this for Estelle, you can do wonders for some of the other escorts.' And then, offering Estelle his arm, he said, 'Shall we go, "Mother"?'

Estelle smiled coyly, took his arm and they walked to his car.

Chapter 22

Colin was so excited about the prospect of seeing Lilly again, and introducing her to his loving 'parents', Aubrey thought the young man was going to wet himself.

'Now, stay calm, son,' he said, actually enjoying the feeling of giving this fatherly advice. Lilly appeared at the Arrivals entrance and Estelle and Aubrey were stunned. She was absolutely beautiful: very tall, slim, elegantly and beautifully dressed in a long silk gown of glowing autumn colours, with a matching turban.

The two young lovers kissed and embraced warmly, and then Colin turned to Estelle and Aubrey and said proudly, 'Lilly, I would like you to meet Estelle and Aubrey, my wonderful parents.'

They all smiled and hugged one another and Lilly kissed both Estelle and Aubrey and said, 'I've been *so* looking forward to meeting you both. Colin has told me so much about you.' And turning to Aubrey she said, 'Colin tells me you are a great dog lover. That is wonderful because I too love dogs, since I was a little girl. I am so looking forward to meeting your little Fritzie.'

Estelle and Aubrey shared a subtle horrified look. But before either had a chance to make any comment, Colin, realising his mistake, because he'd forgotten he'd told her that his previous 'Dad' had a dog, jumped into the conversation saying, 'We'll talk dogs later. Let's get the luggage in the car and get to our hotel.'

'But we are not staying with your mother and father? '

'Oh,' jumped in Estelle, 'you'll be much more comfortable in a hotel … and it's so much more central … And I'm sure, much more private … But we'll have you out to dinner, of course,' she improvised.

'And I can meet your Fritzie then,' laughed Lilly, happily.

'Well,' improvised Aubrey, not to be outdone, 'he hasn't been all that well. We've had to take him to the vet … And it could be serious,' he said, looking at Estelle and Colin, meaningfully.

'Oh, I hope not,' said the lovely Lilly, sadly.

Everything went swimmingly at the hotel, and 'parents' and children got on famously. They had morning tea at the restaurant and Lilly offered them champagne, which both Estelle and Aubrey politely declined, saying it was far too early in the day for alcohol. 'In fact,' admitted Estelle, 'I don't drink at all. It plays up with my … gout. But Aubrey drinks like a fish,' she laughed. 'And gets quite giggly.'

Aubrey scowled.

After they left the hotel for the office, Aubrey and Estelle chatted about the morning events, and felt very pleased with themselves and their clever deception. After a long, thoughtful pause, Estelle said, 'I've just been thinking, Mr Aubrey, we'll probably be seeing quite a lot of Colin and Lilly over the next few days and things could get awkward if Lilly insists on seeing our home. Why don't you pack a few things and leave them at my house so if we take them back there it will look more legitimate – you know, more obvious that we are both living there.'

'That sounds like an excellent idea, Estelle. After all, you did invite them home for dinner one night and, as you say, it will be a bit suspicious if none of my things are in evidence. I'll throw a few things in a suitcase and drop them over later, just in case.'

For the next few days they all had a wonderful time. Aubrey and Estelle took them to Sea World, where Lilly fell in love with the dolphins, and Dreamworld, where she fell in love with the tigers, and Movie World, where she became quite attracted to Batman, until she discovered he was wearing a moulded plastic suit. Aubrey won a huge, stuffed pink French poodle from one of the stalls and presented it to Estelle who was delighted.

They swam in the surf, walked the wonderful beaches, drove the beautiful hinterland with its picturesque gift shops and restaurants, and lay in the sun, which didn't do a thing for Lilly's natural tan but turned Aubrey's face and shoulders into a bright red, sun-baked desert, even after being coated with lotion by Estelle, which only turned him ruddier as she massaged it into his skin.

Meanwhile, back at the office, Penny and Charles were run off their feet with work. Charles was sitting at his desk when Penny rang through, saying there was a very nice-looking man in reception, asking if he could see him. She said he wouldn't give a name but it was about the escort job he'd read about in the paper a while back. She supposed he wanted an interview but she was flat out at the moment, being without Estelle's help, so would he mind seeing him?

Charles sighed, and relented, saying, 'All right, Penny, send him in.'

The door opened and Penny ushered in a very good-looking man in his early forties, tall, with dark, wavy hair and startling blue eyes, apparently well built, with biceps straining the material of his short-sleeved sports shirt, and his well-muscled thighs nicely filling his white sharkskin slacks. Charles looked up with a smile ready to greet the prospective escort, and the smile slowly froze on his face.

'Rodney?' he managed at last, through a suddenly constricting throat. 'Rodney, is that you?'

The handsome man smiled, revealing perfect white teeth and said, 'Hello, Charlie, long time no see.'

Penny withdrew, seeing that obviously the two men knew each other, and closed the door behind her. Charles stood and strode around his desk and embraced the man warmly.

Releasing Rodney, Charles stepped back looking at the younger man, as if seeing a ghost. 'What happened to you? I rang and rang after I found your note at the Club. It appeared that you'd vanished off the face of the earth.'

Rodney shrugged. 'Well, you saw what happened back there. Remember that was the fourth time and I just couldn't take it anymore. That Bray Brothers gang are rough bastards and they weren't going to give up.'

'There was blood on the note,' Charles reminded him. 'I presumed it was yours?'

Rodney nodded.

'My God, were you hurt badly?'

'I survived,' Rodney said philosophically.

Charles sighed. 'This is such a relief. I thought you were dead. I even went to the police and filed a missing person's report. I expected they'd find your body face down in the Thames, and then mine a couple of days later.'

Impulsively, he grabbed Rodney again and hugged him in relief. 'But how did you find me out here?

Rodney smiled. 'I saw you on the telly. You were looking pretty good too.' He looked around the office, taking it all in. 'Well, it seems you're doing very nicely in the Antipodes. A brilliant idea, Charlie, wish we'd thought of it back home. It might've kept the Bray Brothers off our backs.'

'Probably not,' Charles sighed. 'Anyone else making money out of the flesh business would bring out their "protective" instincts, even old wrinkled flesh. So how long do you plan to stay out here?'

Rodney shrugged and smiled that smile again. 'All depends. I'm on a Visiting Businessman's Visa, so I got a while to make up me mind.'

'About what?' asked Charles.

'About you,' said Rodney. He then walked slowly to Charles, wrapped him in his arms and kissed him passionately.

In the front reception, Penny had her own surprise. A solid, maybe even fat, man entered. He was obviously a tourist, being dressed in an expensive, two-piece casual suit and tie, and looking very prosperous. Probably a visiting businessman from the Convention Centre, she thought. They were getting a few of them lately: rich, middle aged, separated from their wives and families; not necessarily looking for sex, but looking for a suitable, respectable lady to accompany them to functions.

'Yes sir, can I help you?' she asked pleasantly.

'I 'ope so,' he replied, in an obviously English accent. 'I'm lookin' for a young lady by the name of Penny Pryce. I take it that's you?'

'Yes,' Penny said curiously. 'I'm Penny Pryce. And you are …?'

'George!' he announced with open arms and a big smile that showed a gold front tooth glittering. 'Your Uncle George! I believe your Mum told you to expect me?'

'Uncle George!' Penny screamed as she ran around the counter to embrace him. 'How wonderful to see you! I wasn't sure you'd get up this far!'

'Well, I was in the neighbourhood, so I fought I'd pop in an' see me little niece,' he said, as he hugged her.

'Oh, this is marvellous!' she said.

They chatted briefly and then Penny grabbed her uncle's hand and dragged him towards Charles' door saying, 'You've just got to meet my boss.'

In her excitement, she burst into Charles' office without knocking as she usually did. 'Mr Charles, you won't believe who ...'

She stopped dead in her tracks surveying the scene in front of her. Charles, eyes closed in rapture, was lying on his back on the floor and the handsome man she'd let in for an 'interview,' was lying on top of him! Rodney looked up in surprise at the sudden interruption.

There was a long embarrassed silence before Rodney finally offered an explanation.

'He had a funny turn and passed out on the floor ... I was just trying to give him mouth-to-mouth resuscitation.'

Penny put her hands on her hips and her eyes rose to the ceiling as she asked dubiously, 'Well, shouldn't your head be up the other end?'

Charles opened his eyes and faked a groan. 'He was just ... checking my pulse ...Thank you, Rodney, I'm feeling much better now.' He eased Rodney off him and they both got to their feet, making sure their backs were towards Penny, as they rearranged themselves.

'Well, well, well,' said Uncle George, smiling in the doorway.

Charles spun around and stared in horror at his nemesis, George Bray!

'Who's a naughty boy then? ... 'Allo, Charlie, good to see you're still hard at it, son.' He laughed uproariously.

Charles turned to look at Rodney, aghast.

To his credit, Rodney hung his head in shame. 'Sorry, Charlie.'

Under the circumstances, Charles did the only thing possible: he fainted.

Chapter 23

'Now, here's the picture, Charlie,' said Uncle George, sitting in the visitor's chair opposite a still shocked Charles. Penny had been discreetly asked to leave the room, and the shame-faced Rodney stood by the door.

'When I saw you on the telly an' saw 'ow well you was doin', I thought to meself, George, I think it's time to go International. I'm sure Charlie-boy would jump at the chance to 'ave you as a partner. Apart from my usual Protective Insurance, I could 'ave an interesting and profitable business coming into Australia. I think young Penny told you I was in the import-export business. Meth, ice, coke, speed – you name it, I can import and supply, guaranteed quality. Yeah,' he chuckled at the prospect, 'I could import the goods and export the money back 'ome.'

Charles went to interrupt but George held up his hand to forestall him, relaxing back in his chair and placing the fingertips of each hand together, but it wasn't in prayer.

'Now, I reckon your oldies could be a good market. After all, it's the oldies that really need the drugs, not the young breed. So, with the right marketing, I reckon we could both be onto a good deal here. What d'you reckon, Charlie?'

Charles swallowed and said, 'Definitely not, George, this is not that sort of business. They're old people, for God's sake. I told you before I wouldn't have anything to do with drugs.'

'Yeah, an' look where that got you, sweatin' away in the tropics an' runnin' an old people's 'ome.

Charles looked at Rodney by the door. Rodney shook his head sadly, trying to avoid Charles' stare.

'And I take it Rodney switched sides, right? He wasn't beaten up and threatened at all, was he? He was working for you.'

'No! That's not right, Charlie,' Rodney blurted out. 'Not at the start. That last night when they showed up, they did threaten me and carve me up a bit; they scared the shit outa me. It was either join them on the spot and go along with them, or die an ugly death. I didn't have any other option.'

'He still doesn't,' said George amiably. 'And I must say, he's been very … useful. My own PBS.'

'Private Businessman's Secretary?' scoffed Charles.

'No, Personal Bum-boy Security,' George corrected him.

Charles glanced again at Rodney who stood, looking downcast, and mortally ashamed.

'I didn't want to do it, Charlie …'

'… but you had no choice,' Charles finished for him.

Rodney nodded his head.

Charles looked at George, defeated.

'You're an evil bastard, George. I suppose the pattern's going to have to repeat itself again, right?'

173

'Yeah,' George agreed with him. 'Business as usual. I've already sussed the place out, an' it's going to be only too easy to pick up a couple of bright young lads around 'ere to help me out when I need 'em.' He spread his hands out in front of him to indicate an imagined newspaper headline. *"The Bray Bros. Gang Goes International".* It'll be just like the old times, Charlie, but this time, it'll be in the lovely warm sun. I may even immigrate.'

There was a long painful pause while Charles considered this horrific possibility and his options, then he finally relented. 'All right, George, I know the system.' He paused, searching quickly for some diversion to give him time to think. 'But I've got to have samples, and it'll take a bit of time to spread the word.'

'Samples I can do, but time is short, Charlie. I can only give you a coupla days to make an initial order.'

Charles nodded despondently.

'Oh, an' Charlie,' said George, rising from his seat. 'You wouldn't think of doing anything silly, would you? I mean, if you did I'd just have to take you and Rodney, and maybe even my lovely niece out there, on a long fishing trip, say, trolling for sharks. I hear you got some nice hungry ones out here – what are they called? Bull sharks?'

He laughed to himself as he headed for the door, which Rodney opened for him. 'You should appeal to them, Charlie, 'cause they'd be used to being full of bullshit.' This made him laugh even louder as he headed out the door. 'Be in touch.'

Rodney gave Charles a final sad look and followed.

Charles hung his head in both hands and sat, staring at his desk. After a moment, there was a soft knock at the door and Penny entered. 'Charlie, I was standing outside the door listening. I'm *so* sorry. I told you I didn't know much about him, he's me Mum's brother. They're from the weird side of the family.'

She stepped up to his desk. 'What are we going to do?'

Charles took his time to look up at her and said, 'I don't know, Penny, but there's one thing for sure, I'm not getting stuck with the bloody Bray Brothers again.'

He absently rubbed his chin as he thought. 'Well, one thing's for sure, I can't go back to England. I couldn't move in with Lord Swindon, that'd be almost worse than your Uncle George. The Lady Celia wouldn't have me back, and even if she did, that would certainly be worse than your Uncle George, and I'm not bloody well moving to Japan as a house guest of the Sumo wrestler and his sparring partner. And, most of all, I can't leave all of you to face the disaster. Maybe we could all move to India and join Aub's mother in the ashram.'

Penny shook her head. 'I look shockin' in a sari, anyway.' Then she smiled gently. 'But maybe you'd look good.'

Charles looked embarrassed. 'Sorry about, you know, catching me like that. It must've been a terrible shock.'

'Oh, it doesn't bother me, Charlie, just don't do it in broad daylight on the beach and frighten the seagulls. I'd guessed about you a long time ago anyway. Did you think I thought you dragged me 'round the clubs to help you pick up women? Nah, it was 'cause I attracted men. I may be blonde but I ain't stupid.'

'No, that wasn't the case, I promise you, Penny. Anyway, any good-looking man attracted to you wouldn't give a rat's arse about an old poof like me.' He returned to the subject in hand. 'What the hell am I going to do?'

'Now the battle isn't over till the fat lady dances,' she said, happily mixing metaphors, even though she didn't actually know what a metaphor was. But she sure knew what a fat lady was; Bianca for one. 'I'm going to make you a nice cup of tea, and we can both think what we're going to do about this schemozzle.'

'Thank you, Penny, and I really mean thank you. Even if I don't know what a schemozzle is.'

Penny smiled and left the office.

'Estelle?' Penny said into the phone, conspiratorially. 'You and Mr Aubrey have got to get back here as soon as you can. We've got another disaster on our hands, and this time I really mean a disaster. This one makes the Delilah and Joshua episode look like a tea party. – Well, yes, I know it was but I mean this is really big. – Drugs! – Yes, I said drugs! Uncle George turned out to be Mr Charles's enemy from London, George Bray! And he was here! He threatened to feed Mr Charles to the sharks if he didn't pay protection money and push drugs, and I don't mean antihistamines! – No, not in the clubs or on the street. Here, to the geriatric escorts!'

She hung up the phone and said to herself, 'There, that should get them off the water slide at Wet 'n' Wild.'

Chapter 24

It was the last day of Lilly and Colin's holiday and Estelle had got carried away and invited the couple over to her home for a farewell dinner before they left the next day for England. Aubrey had done as she suggested, and moved a few of his things into her house as window dressing, and she would prepare a lovely dinner party.

The only other problem was that Joshua had been taken to hospital that morning due to a relapse. He was having blackouts and the doctors were worried that he might have more damage than they first suspected from the morning tea and skillet episode. He would only be in overnight, but still feeling a little guilty about the disastrous tea party, Estelle offered to let Fritzie stay the night at her house.

In a way, that would be good because Lilly could then meet the monster she was so persistent in talking about, which would most likely put her off dogs for life. Fritzie would be securely tied to the Hills Hoist in the backyard, with a blanket to sleep on. And anyway, she thought, it's only for the one night.

Then she got the phone call on her mobile, indeed, while she and Aubrey were experiencing the Big Dipper at Wet 'n' Wild, and shouted her concern to Aubrey over the noise of the other screaming tourists. Several young people overheard her yelling, 'Drugs! – Drugs!' as they slid down over the second hump and by the time they'd reached the pool at the bottom, a scruffy young man sidled up to them and muttered, 'Yeah, what ya got an' how much?'

They made quick excuses to Lilly and Colin, saying Fritzie wasn't well, and they'd have to take him to the vet. Lilly and Colin were quite upset and understood their concern. They urged the 'parents' to go straight home, and they would get a bus back to their hotel, and see them later that evening for dinner. Lilly insisted they ring them if the dinner would be inconvenient.

In the car on their way back to the office, Aubrey and Estelle discussed the limited information Estelle had received from the obviously distraught Penny, and were shocked at the implications.

How could it be possible that Penny's Uncle George turned out to be the English gangster, George Bray? And what could be done about it? How did he know Charles was in Australia, and where to find him?

Aubrey immediately remembered the television interview and sighed, 'That's the price you pay for fame. If only I hadn't been so good, the BBC would never have picked it up!'

Estelle politely ignored the remark and tried to concentrate on a solution to their problem. 'It would have to happen today of all days,' she complained. 'At least tomorrow we have a free day after Lilly and Colin leave.'

'It's probably a storm in a teacup,' Aubrey said.

'Please don't use that expression, Mr. Aubrey,' Estelle replied.

When they arrived at the office, all four of them went directly into the conference room to discuss the problem. Charles explained most of what had happened, and Penny filled them in on everything else, except of course, for Charles being caught in *flagrante delicto*, or in this case, in flagrante dick-lickto, with Rodney.

After a few moments of highly concentrated thought, Estelle suddenly said, 'Leave it to me. I might just have a solution.' She wouldn't expound upon her idea, she said, until she checked it out, finalised and confirmed the plan. But she needed to know exactly when Uncle George contacted Charles with the details of the 'drop'. In the meantime, they were all to keep thinking of alternative options in case Estelle's plan didn't crystallise.

Estelle and Aubrey then collected the wretched Fritzie, who was, at the time, humping his live-in lover, the vinyl chair, on the back deck, threw him in Aubrey's car, and drove to Estelle's house. Fritzie was securely tethered to the Hills Hoist and given a bowl of water and a blanket to lie on, which he immediately set about shredding.

The dinner party that evening was most successful and for a while Aubrey and Estelle didn't have time to think of their business problems. The platter of Oysters Natural, followed by the Mud Crab Bisque, Baked Snapper and Greek Salad, topped off with Estelle's

180

special Crème Caramel and after-dinner coffee (with mints, of course), was a delight enjoyed by the whole company. The conversation flowed with the excellent wine Colin had kindly provided, with Estelle imbibing only a single small glass for the toasting of the young couple's future life together.

And then came the 'Grande Surprise'. Lilly had decided they should check out of their hotel and, with Estelle and Aubrey's permission, of course, spend their last night in Australia with their loving 'parents'! For Lilly and Colin, this would be the perfect ending, she said, of their wonderful holiday, made possible by the kindness and love of her new-found Mother and Father.

Aubrey looked to Colin in genuine shock and amazement for assurance that this was indeed a joke, and Colin smiled nervously saying he had tried to ring several times but their mobiles weren't switched on. This, of course, was true, as both Estelle and Aubrey had turned off their mobiles while they were in conference with Penny and Charles and, in the confusion of impending doom, had forgotten to turn the phones back on. But Colin assured them that he realised it would be inconvenient and that they were both quite prepared to stay the night at another hotel, closer to the airport.

'But we will be no trouble,' Lilly assured them, 'and I see that you do in fact have a spare room, and second bathroom, and I promise we will clean up after ourselves. You will never know that we were here. It is just that I have grown to love you both so dearly, and would love to spend our last night under the same roof, in my second home, with my second family.'

Aubrey's discomfort was obvious as Colin tried desperately to convince Lilly that they would be imposing, which would be very inconsiderate of them. Lilly suddenly became quite contrite, and almost on the verge of tears, apologised for her thoughtlessness, saying she'd been carried away with all the excitement, and to please forgive her.

'Don't be ridiculous,' said Estelle, 'we'd be delighted to have you both stay for the night.'

Aubrey's jaw dropped in shock and amazement. 'But …' he blurted out, realising he hadn't packed his pyjamas or fresh underpants and socks, and most importantly, he would have to share the bedroom with Estelle!

Estelle silenced him with a look. 'So, that's decided. Of course you must stay.'

Lilly almost cried in her gratitude. Colin, and Aubrey almost died of embarrassment. Estelle, of course, handled the whole thing with great equanimity. She shooed the couple out into the back yard to play with 'the delightful Fritzie', as Lilly lovingly dubbed the ugly mongrel, saying she and 'Father' would do the dishes.

As soon as the young couple departed, Aubrey immediately bombarded Estelle with his whispered concerns but she simply turned to him, as she cleared away the last of the dinner crockery, and said, 'Now don't be silly, Aubrey, we are two intelligent mature people. We're certainly capable of behaving in a civilised way. And besides, it will give Lilly so much pleasure. Is it too much to ask?'

'No, I suppose not,' he stammered, after a pause, 'but I didn't pack my 'jamies!'

'Well, sleep in your clothes,' she dismissed his concern.

'I can't sleep fully clothed!' he protested, horrified.

'Well, sleep fully naked,' she replied. 'It's not going to bother me. You can sleep on the floor if you like,' she added a little testily, 'wrapped in a blanket, or barbed wire, if that will make your "vulnerability" any easier to bear.'

'I didn't mean that,' he replied, a little shame-faced. 'I wasn't worried that ...' His voice died out. 'Of course, you're right. I'm just being silly. Forgive me, Ms Twigdon.'

'Forgiven, Mr Aubrey. Now, I'll just see to the fresh towels in the second bathroom.'

The house was quiet except for the mumbled sounds of erotica coming from the second bedroom. Aubrey, in his Jockey Y-fronts and wrapped in a blanket, lay on his back on the far side of the bed, as far away from the apparently sleeping Estelle as possible.

There was no way he was going to be able to sleep, and he lay there with his eyes wide open, staring into the darkness.

The happy young couple had retired for the evening to their room and eventually, after a long, rather tense silence between Estelle and Aubrey, she said, 'Well, I think I'll turn in.' Aubrey jumped at the sudden statement. 'I'll go in first and get undress– ready for bed, and you can follow in a little while, when I put the light out, all right?'

He nodded, nervously.

He'd crept into the darkness of the room, like a cat seeking its haven of invisibility. In the dim moonlight that radiated through the window, he noticed Estelle had her eyes closed, for which he was entirely grateful and quietly slipped out of his clothes, which he left close at hand, in case of fire, on the bedroom chair, next to the pink stuffed poodle he'd given Estelle. He tiptoed to the bed and gently lowered his body to the mattress, easing himself into a rigid supine position, and lay there, wide awake.

Suddenly, his mobile started vibrating, but this time, on the bedside table. He quickly fumbled in the semi-darkness, pushed the connect button, and whispered, 'Hello?'

'Hello, Aubrey, darling? It's Mumsie.'

'Mumsie?' he whispered, desperately glancing over at the sleeping Estelle, 'Where are you? Still in India?'

'Yes, darling, but I'm leaving tomorrow for Machu Picchu.'

'Where?'

'Machu Picchu! South America! We're flying to Lima, and taking a train to Cusco, and then onto Machu Picchu. Isn't it exciting? I've met some wonderful people up here. They're so spiritual. I'm a new woman. And a few of us are going, as a party, to worship and meditate at the Inca temple up there. We'll have to take our own champagne though.'

'Oh, Mumsie,' sighed Aubrey, in despair.

'Why are you whispering, Aubrey?'

'It's one o'clock in the morning and I'm in bed with someone.'

'With someone? In bed? You?' she screamed, forcing Aubrey to hold the phone away from his ear. 'Who are you in bed with? A woman?' she asked incredulously.

'Well, yes, of course it's a woman. I am a grown man, Mumsie.'

'Oh no, darling, I'm not annoyed, I'm just a bit ... surprised. Who is she? Is it serious? Will you be getting married?' she asked hopefully.

'No, of course not! It's not like that, Mumsie. Look, it's very difficult to talk right now so you'll have to ring me back when you get to ... wherever it is you're going.'

'Machu Picchu.'

'Right, then call me when you get there, all right?'

'Of course, darling. Sorry to disturb your lovely tryst. I'll ring you later. Just wanted you to know where I'll be if you need me. Goodbye darling ... and, Aubrey, you are wearing a condom, aren't you?'

'I won't be needing one, Mumsie. It's not what ... Oh, what's the use. I'll talk to you later.' And with that, he disconnected the line.

About an hour later, Aubrey had finally drifted off to sleep and was snoring softly. Out in the back yard, completely forgotten, Fritzie had just returned from exploring the neighbourhood. Lilly and Colin had neglected to tie him back to the clothes hoist after playing with him, and they had returned to the house, also forgetting to secure the back door.

Fritzie soon sniffed out the situation and decided to take the opportunity to explore the *interior* neighbourhood. He nosed open the back door and, in the silent darkness, padded through the house, looking for company. The door to one bedroom was closed, so he extended his exploration until he came upon a door that was only pulled to and slightly ajar. Again he nosed it gently and it silently swung inwards.

To his delight, he perceived a large double bed that was obviously occupied by not one, but two sleeping bodies! What luck! He hunched his hips and leaped.

He achieved a magnificent four-point landing on the tarmac of Aubrey's tummy!

With the sudden shock of Fritzie's arrival on his unprotected stomach, Aubrey farted loudly and shot into the air like a rocket leaving the pad at Cape Canaveral. But the booster failed, and he fell back to Earth into the outstretched arms of an equally shocked, but not entirely unwillingly, Estelle.

For a seemingly endless moment they shared a startled stare and then, inevitably, came the slow ignition of desire, as Aubrey's rocket uncontrollably readied itself for re-launch.

'Oh, Mr. Aubrey,' Estelle murmured in quivering anticipation.

'Oh, Estelle,' Aubrey responded breathlessly.

186

At first tentatively and then hungrily they sought each other's eager lips and bodies, and within moments they were both in orbit and flying through the stars. In the ensuing fervour Fritzie was unceremoniously flung from the bed and landed on the pink stuffed poodle in the corner.

He immediately responded enthusiastically to the challenge.

'Ah, ma cherie,' he growled seductively.

Later when all were spent, Aubrey lay on his back, smiling contentedly in the afterglow of unbelievable ecstasy.

Cuddled into his shoulder, Estelle slept, peaceful as an angel. But inside, the Devil had finally awoken.

And Fritzie lay exhausted on the floor, his front paw looped over the pink stuffed poodle, thinking, These French chicks sure know their business.

Chapter 25

The next morning, a newly invigorated and happy Estelle and Aubrey dropped Lilly and Colin off at the airport, and with loving hugs and warm kisses, they bade them farewell. Lilly and Estelle cried of course, but Aubrey and Colin shook hands formally and gave each other a perfunctory embrace. Colin whispered in Aubrey's ear, 'You were both marvellous. I've written the cheque out, and I included the cost of a hotel room for the night, and the superb meal – and added a little bonus for you and Mum. It's in your jacket pocket. We'll never forget our time with you – Dad.'

'Neither will we,' Aubrey whispered back, 'believe me – son.'

Colin gave his arm an extra little squeeze and said, 'Remember, anytime you're in England, you're more than welcome to stay with us.'

'Thank you,' said Aubrey. 'We might even bring Fritzie with us.'

On the way back to the office, nothing was said about the previous night's intimate encounter, but a warm, relaxed relationship existed between them. Estelle related the plan she had in mind to frustrate Uncle George's attempts to destroy their happy and successful business and Aubrey, although very concerned about the safety and success of the scheme, conceded it was certainly worth a try. Estelle had phoned Penny with the instructions, and Penny had passed the information on to Charles. And now they just had to wait until the right time presented itself.

The time came sooner than they expected. Uncle George rang Charles with his demands and told him that he and his 'friends' would arrive that afternoon at three o'clock. Charles reminded him, in his best Humphrey Bogart voice, that the samples better be good or there would be no deal, regardless of his threats. He assured Uncle George that, since their experience in London, he had 'wised up', and had his own gang of heavies at his disposal, and if the deal was screwed up, a gangland war would erupt that would 'blow open' the whole of the Gold Coast. Uncle George was wary but respectful of this newly experienced adversary.

At the appointed time, Uncle George and four of his recently acquired local hoods turned up at the agency office. Two of the hoods stood guard outside, while Uncle George, a reluctant Rodney, and the two other hoods entered the Reception area.

The two hoods wore alpine-patterned balaclavas and held one hand in a suspiciously bulging pocket of their ski jackets. They must've been steaming hot, as it was thirty degrees outside.

They removed their weapons from their pockets as soon as they stepped inside the door, and closing it behind them, pointed the guns threateningly at the terrified Estelle and Penny.

Uncle George said, 'Sorry about this, ladies, but if you just keep nice and shtum, and lead us into Charlie's office, nobody need get hurt. This is not a hold-up, this is a business deal.'

The two women rose from their chairs and, with their hands raised in the air, led the way nervously to the office.

The door opened and the protagonists came face to face.

'Hello, George. Don't think you've met my partner, Aubrey Acres,' said Charles mildly, and apparently very much in control. 'Aubrey, this is the not-so-lovely George – George Bray, an ex-business acquaintance from London, and another ex-friend, the definitely lovely Rodney.'

Aubrey nodded, hardly covering his nervousness.

'I won't say it's a pleasure,' squeaked Aubrey, who just failed in making it sound confident.

'So, let's get down to business, shall we, gentlemen?' said Charles, maintaining his 'crime boss' manner, 'Do sit down and make yourselves comfortable.'

The two hoons at the door stood motionless.

'No?' said Charles, 'As you wish.'

Uncle George accepted the invitation to sit, while the others stood.

'Shall I make tea?' Estelle offered weakly as she made a step towards the desk. 'I've already made a pot for Mr Charles, but I could easily make another.'

'I don't think that will be necessary, Ms Twigdon,' Aubrey answered.

'No,' said Charles. 'They may suspect we're trying to poison them.' He laughed evilly. 'Now George, let's have the samples, eh?'

Uncle George felt a little uneasy at this new attitude of Charles' and looked around the room for a trap. Seeing none, he cautiously withdrew a few small plastic bags from his suit pocket and laid them on the desk in front of Charles.

'I picked these up this morning from my supplier. He assures me he is carrying a sizeable stock in hand and delivery will be supplied in pizza boxes'.

'Pizza boxes,' smirked Charles. 'How original.'

'And, of course, the cash will be paid on delivery of the merchandise,' George added, smiling, 'with, of course, the protection insurance premium.'

'Of course,' said Charles, 'as has always been your MO.'

Aubrey couldn't help raising his eyebrow at all this gangland dialogue. Charles pretended to taste the 'samples' as he had seen so often in the movies. He laid them back down on the desk, looked at Aubrey and nodded. 'It's the good stuff, all right. What do you think?'

Aubrey repeated his nervous nod, not trusting his voice to speak.

'All right, George, you crafty old bastard, we have a deal,' said Charles, as he held out his hand for Uncle George to shake.

As they shook hands Charles 'accidentally' manoeuvred the hand-shake towards the teapot on the desk and knocked it, causing it to crash loudly to the floor.

The two hoods at the door stepped forwards protectively but it was too late. The signal had been given.

Within seconds, the door was flung open and the room filled with a seething mass of Grey Power, like a volcano erupting, and spewing a mass of grey, and occasionally tinted, 'ash power' over the enemy. As per Estelle's plan, the residents and many of the escorts had all congregated in the conference room earlier, armed to the teeth, waiting for the prearranged signal of the crashing teapot, and on the signal, had charged out of the conference room and into the office like a pack of screaming banshees.

Almost every tenant and every old escort had responded to the call to arms. In all, there seemed to be dozens of them including Arthur bringing up the rear with his new walker.

Like a sea of molten lava, they swamped the criminal invaders who threatened their tranquil home, their peaceful way of life, not to mention their pocket money. They had armed themselves with any deadly, lethal weapon they could find: kitchen cutting boards, rolling pins, pots and pans, lamp bases, garden tools, electric irons, golf clubs, never-used fire irons they'd brought with them when they moved north from Melbourne; all manner of Weapons of Mass Destruction.

Beryl-nee-Bianca brandished her .38 revolver, and Alexander the Great sported his 'roo-shooting rifle, a

Winchester .300 WSM. Anthony was armed with his trusty fish gaff.

The two remaining hoons, hearing the screaming commotion inside, ran in and joined the melee but were quickly set upon by the aging defenders and disarmed.

Delilah was brandishing her trusty skillet and Joshua, now released from hospital, brought the Hound from Hell, Fritzie, but they both steered clear of Delilah, who single-handedly threw herself on the nearest hoon, knocked him to the floor with her lethal skillet, and whipped off his balaclava. 'Jeremy Forbes!' she screamed, obviously recognising him, 'you naughty little boy! You just wait until I see your mother.'

In the midst of the chaos, Rodney took his long-awaited revenge on George, grabbed him, and landed a few solid punches. Charles, neatly ducking a wayward blow from Raoul-nee-Fred, who had got a little carried away and was swinging his rolling pin at anything that moved, saw this, and ran to Rodney to assist. Rodney turned the luckless George around to face Charles and said, 'Be my guest.'

With great pleasure, Charles drew back his arm and punched George squarely in the nose, breaking it, and spurting blood over Charles' new white shirt. 'Bugger!' Charles said, as he tried wiping off the blood with his handkerchief. The two men smiled at each other in satisfaction and embraced.

Penny cowered in the corner protecting her nail varnish from the onslaught, but Estelle threw herself into the battle with great fervour, accidentally knocking out two of the luckless tenants, before being physically restrained by Aubrey, who turned her around, looked at her with loving pride, and kissed her firmly on the lips.

The rather one-sided battle seemed to rage for ever when, in fact, it only took a very short time before the sound of police sirens could be heard above the clamour. Penny raised her manicured fingers to her lips and gave a piercing whistle, as a signal that the battle had been won and the troops were to disperse. The noise and clamour slowly receded and the combatants dissolved out through the door, dragging their wounded, to return quietly to their previously mundane existence.

'Thanks, guys,' she yelled as they dispersed. 'See you all at the celebration party.'

By the time the police arrived, George and four of his gang were lying on the floor, well trounced, and bound with office Sellotape.

The police officer who had been previously alerted of the attempted drug deal, stood over the bound five men, shaking his head in disbelief. 'Do you mean to tell me that you five,' he said pointing at Estelle, Penny, Aubrey, Charles and Rodney, 'overcame these five gentlemen by yourselves?'

'Well, that's only one apiece,' said Estelle. 'They were pussies, a push-over.'

'Thank God you're 'ere,' Uncle George ranted at the police officer. 'Get me the fook away from those fookin' Varicose Vigilantes. They're fookin' barmy.'

The officer walked over to the desk and picked up the drug samples, looked at them, and turned to Uncle George. 'You're here under a tourist visa, I take it, sir?'

Uncle George nodded dolefully.

'Well, I'd say, after this little effort, you won't be visiting our shores again, sir. You'll probably serve a sentence, to be decided by the officiating Magistrate, and then be deported to your country of origin. That'd be Ireland, right?'

'Fookin' England!' retorted an outraged Uncle George.

'Same thing,' shrugged the officer. 'Come on.'

'Deportation out of this fookin' 'olding pen for undertakers will be a fookin' pleasure!' groaned Uncle George, as they led him away.

'Oh, by the way, Uncle George,' Penny called as they departed, 'Give my love to me Mum when she comes to visit you. Tell her I'll call when I get the chance.'

Uncle George scowled and muttered, 'Fook ya fookin' mother 'n all,' as the five prisoners were led out to the waiting police van.

Chapter 26

The wedding was a simple affair. They'd decided on a Marriage Celebrant named Tanya Turnbull, and the ceremony was held in the garden of the apartment block. Neither Estelle nor Aubrey wanted a church wedding, or anything too formal, and the reception was also held in the garden, decorated to perfection by Charles and Rodney, in pink and white, which Delilah definitely approved of. Estelle thought the garden an ideal setting as it would be easier for some of the tenants and escorts to get there, and also cheaper than catching a bus or train, even with their Pensioner Concession cards.

Estelle's mother was present of course, accompanied by two burly keepers dressed as nurses. She behaved herself remarkably well and only once did she have to be restrained, and that was when she dropped to her hands and knees, barked and tried to bite Fritzie. But Joshua-nee-Joe threw her a Frisbee and that kept her and Fritzie entertained for the rest of the ceremony. It was only when she tried to pee up against the trunk of the *eucalypt aggregata* that the handlers moved in.

Estelle chose a lovely pale grey chiffon ensemble, rather than going for the traditional virginal white, which, by now, she considered inappropriate. The bridesmaid, Penny of course, looked lovely in a yellow flowing chiffon model. Aubrey and his best man, Charles, wore matching pale grey suits and shirts with yellow ties. Rodney offered to be flower-girl but Estelle declined his kind offer, stating she didn't want to be upstaged by a poof in a dress.

Estelle and Aubrey had discussed the revelation that Charles had 'escaped from the wardrobe', as Estelle put it, but she was quite accepting, saying she wasn't a bit surprised as it did explain some of Mr Charles' peculiarities. On the other hand, Aubrey was a little mystified, saying, 'Maybe that's why Charles had been so popular at Timbertop. It never occurred to me. I just thought he was very British.'

Just before the service began, Charles and a very nervous Aubrey were standing under an arch of multi-coloured flowers, at the spot where the service was to take place, waiting for the bride's entrance. Aubrey turned and smiled at the guests, all seated in white plastic armchairs decorated with pink satin bows, many of whom waved and smiled back. Suddenly a vision in a pure white, floor-length silk robe and matching headscarf bejewelled with glittering rhinestones, appeared at the back of the aisle, arm in arm with a tall, blonde, muscular and very handsome young man.

Aubrey gasped, causing Charles to turn around and also see the vision of loveliness. 'My God,' said Charles, 'he's a cute one,' at which Rodney scowled jealously.

'Not him,' gasped Aubrey, 'Her! … It's Mumsie!'

He literally flew down the aisle and threw his arms around her in unbridled joy. 'Mumsie, you made it! I'm so happy!'

'Did you think I'd miss my own little boy's wedding?' she laughed, patting him on the head. 'I just had to meet my new daughter-in-law and the woman brave enough to take you on.'

'This is marvellous! How long are you staying for, Mumsie?'

'Oh, just for a couple of days, darling. Ricardo and I are on our way to a spiritual retreat in New Zealand.' She turned and introduced her escort, 'Aubrey, this is Ricardo, he's Swedish and only speaks a little English, but that doesn't matter when you're spiritually conjoined, does it?'

Before he could answer, the three-piece chamber music trio segued into 'Here Comes the Bride'. Aubrey kissed his mother, saying they'd talk at the reception, and flew back down the aisle to await his fate.

When the Celebrant asked, 'Who gives this woman to be joined in legal wedlock to this man,' the entire congregation rose, as one, and said, 'We do!'

At the end of the service, the bride and groom kissed chastely, and the entire congregation burst into cheers and applause.

The reception went off brilliantly and Estelle got to meet her new mother-in-law, who laughingly volunteered humiliating stories about Aubrey's childhood, to his great embarrassment, and to Estelle's delight. Daisy/Pomegranate also talked of meeting Ricardo at the art classes she had attended in Zurich, which prompted Aubrey to remark, 'I didn't know you'd taken up painting, Mumsie?'

To which Ricardo replied, in heavily accented English, 'She vasn't painting, she vas modelling, for zee Life classes. She made zee Mona Lisa look like, how you say, a plate of Sviss Strudel.'

Everyone laughed except Aubrey, who blushed in mortification. Estelle slipped her hand around his waist, let it drift down to his bottom, and gave it a cheeky pinch.

Epilogue

They honeymooned in England, leaving Charles, Rodney and Penny in charge of the apartments and the Twilight Escort Agency. Of course, Estelle and Aubrey were able to attend Colin and Lilly's wedding and meet Lilly's vast extended family, who treated the 'Australian parents' with great respect and friendliness. Aubrey even talked confidentially to Colin about the possibility of actually adopting him legally.

When they returned home several weeks later, a very excited Charles, Rodney and Penny picked them up from the airport and made a slight detour into the centre of Surfers Paradise, insisting that Aubrey and Estelle keep their eyes closed until they were told they could open them. Finally the car pulled to a stop. Charles and Rodney helped them out, and led them, like a blind couple, to the footpath. Standing side by side they were then allowed to open their eyes, and told to look up.

Aubrey and Estelle followed the instructions, and gasped in astonishment.

There before them was a very smart, modern establishment, decorated with frescos of near-naked young men wearing nothing but Stetsons, and subtle phallic symbols. Over the front door, ablaze with flashing neon light tubes, was a very provocative sign which read: